THE LOST

TALES OF THE FEISTY DRUID™ BOOK 5

CANDY CRUM

MICHAEL ANDERLE

From Candy

To my boys, thank you for
being my reason for everything.
To my family who support me
no matter what.
To the fans and readers--thank you!

From Michael

To Family, Friends and
Those Who Love
To Read.
May We All Enjoy Grace
To Live The Life We Are
Called.

The Undying Illusionist Team

JIT / Beta Readers

Kimberly Boyer
Kelly O'Donnell
John Findlay
Daniel Weigert
Larry Omans
Micky Cocker
Alex Wilson
Tim Bischoff

Thomas Ogden
Joshua Ahles
Paul Westman

If we missed anyone, please let us know!

Editor
Lynne Stiegler

THE LOST

It was hard for Arryn to believe that her journey in Arcadia had ended for the time being, and not even remotely close to the way she had expected. The hardships there hadn't killed her desire to go back to the city for good, or to do good things there, but there were things she had to do before setting foot within the walls again.

At least for any purpose other than a visit to Amelia.

In the beginning, when she had first planned to go back to Arcadia, she wanted to get back there and make sure the people there were doing well, and work to make things better however she could.

Even Cathillian had wanted to help, which she found amusing. Before they arrived, she would have bet he would end up spending the majority of his time wandering the city and flirting—but she would have been wrong. She and Cathillian had set out to do great things: teaching at the Academy, training soldiers, training civilians in nature magic to help them better gather resources, and other things.

But more than anything, Arryn's number-one purpose for

going back had been to find her father, or at least find out what had happened to him. She had wanted to find any and all clues that might lead her to find him, but except for a single conversation with Elon, there hadn't been anything to find. However, that one conversation had been very informative.

If everything Elon had said was true—and she had no reason to believe he had lied—it looked as though the dark druids had taken him. More specifically, Aeris.

Though there wasn't any way for her to prove it, her instincts weren't usually wrong.

When she had first come to the Dark Forest, Aeris hadn't been shy about his hatred for her. Her arrival had driven him mad. To him, the druids were the elite, the best-trained warriors in Irth. They were the ones who practiced the purest form of magic.

In fact, they were supposed to be everything the Arcadians weren't. Brave. Powerful. In tune with life and nature. They had dominion over everything around them. No one was allowed to cross their borders, and their laws were absolute.

Only that was never how it was supposed to be.

The Chieftain had never meant for the Forest to be secluded, segregated from the outside world and uninviting to any who should approach its walls. He wanted it to be a peaceful, beautiful place open to anyone who wanted to live a different kind of life.

The Chieftain was a wise man, one who saw the need for rules and laws, but also knew there were times to break them.

That was why he had taken Arryn in. She had been an innocent child, one who had been raised by kind, loving people. Specifically, by a woman who had been willing to risk her life for that of his grandson.

On the day when Cathillian's life was threatened by a lycanthrope in the Forest, and she had put her own safety aside to save him—a child she had never met and had no responsibility for—he saw Adrien was not a reflection of all the people in his city. There were some who still believed in simple common decency.

The Chieftain saw a beautiful light and potential for great power in Arryn, just as Elysia had, and so he had allowed his daughter to bring the Arcadian girl within their borders.

But Aeris saw that as breaking a law that should have been unconditional—no outsiders.

Hell, if Aeris had known the Chieftain had left the Dark Forest completely in the hands of an outsider while they went to war with Arcadia recently, the deranged dark druid would have burned everything down himself.

He was so prejudiced against the outside world—mainly due to the biased upbringing his parents had provided—that he had developed an intense hatred for the Chieftain for what he had done. Aeris had left the sanctuary of their villages to join the dark druids.

That was why Arryn had no qualms about believing he would be capable of abducting her father.

Who else had the death touch and could move through Arcadia like an assassin, killing every guard he found to get to Christopher, her father? Who else would have hunted him down to remove him from the city?

No one else had known his location. No one else who had magical abilities like his, anyway. That kind of power sure as hell didn't exist in the Arcadians.

Arryn knew what he had done, and the time was getting closer for her to confront him face to face. The immediate danger for Arcadia was over, and the city was back in capable hands. Now it was time for Arryn to focus on her home in the Forest.

She would soon see Aeris. She would soon face his Dark Chieftain. She only hoped his horrible brother, Jerick, would be with him. That way she could get revenge on Aeris for what he had done to her father, on the dark chieftain on the behalf of the people of the Dark Forest, and on Jerick for what he had allowed to happen to Corrine.

Though Arryn had no way of knowing what her future held, there was something deeply satisfying about the thought of going head to head with Aeris. And she knew that time would come very, *very* soon.

CHAPTER ONE

Sitting around the campfire with her friends and family, Arryn felt a sense of contentment and happiness. Everything had worked out in the end, and somehow, they had all managed to survive.

For the time being, they were able to relax, though the threat of the dark druids marching directly east from the Terres Forest instead of moving south to avoid the Dark Forest was still there.

The patrol had been increased the moment they had returned from Arcadia, and they had already made plans to intercept them if that were to happen. But for now, the Chieftain was satisfied Alaric wouldn't be so stupid.

Not many people really knew what had happened all those years ago, and because of that, the Chieftain decided a history lesson was in order. It was true that his people would fight for him without question. They always had, knowing they were fighting for a good man with a pure heart.

But young Corrine had asked about the origin story. "What happened with you, Alaric, and Jerick? Why do they hate you so much?"

It had no doubt been confusion that prompted the inquiry. Given where she had grown up and the terrible things she had probably heard from people, she had learned never to trust. It must have created a great curiosity in her when she met the true Chieftain—the first of his title.

The Chieftain had now decided everyone deserved to know exactly who they fought and why. They deserved to know why their home would be threatened *again*, and why he would need them to defend it.

The Chieftain prepared to speak, and Zoe's eyes turned white. The young mystic was looking forward to giving the druids of the Dark Forest a show to enhance their leader's story. She believed this story was worthy of it, and the Chieftain had agreed.

He allowed her access to his mind, letting her see the things he would recall as he spoke. The faces. The Forest. And though the druids were wary of mystical magic, especially given the battle they had just fought, they found themselves excited to experience what she had offered.

Zoe had gone into Arcadia with them with no real battle training at all, and had risked her life to help Arryn take down Scarlett and the others. She had earned her place among them.

The Chieftain took a drink from one of his two mugs of wine. Arryn had finally discovered why he carried both. It wasn't the obvious—that he had a problem. No, it was because he made two types and could never choose between the sweet or the tart, so he chose both.

She had quietly laughed at him as she settled between Cathillian and Elysia, who had taken Zoe's place when she had gone to stand near the Chieftain to provide optimal visibility for everyone.

The Chieftain cleared his throat. "All right, where do I begin? I suppose at the very beginning. It will take a while to get through it, but I guess there's no harm in us having a good story around the fire for a couple of nights, right?"

Everyone smiled and nodded, whispering amongst themselves as they got comfortable. "From the beginning" meant starting with the Founder, Selah, and even Adrien. It meant learning where each man had come from. Even Arryn was on the edge of her seat.

"Our story started over forty years ago, when the Dark Forest was simply an extension of the Terres Forest. These forests belonged to no one and everyone. Arcadia didn't exist. There were only scattered groups of people trying to find their way during an incredibly hard time—the Age of Madness."

THE MOMENT the Chieftain mentioned the Age of Madness, all eyes focused on him even more intently than they had before. Most in the village had no or very little recollection of that time. The majority of the druids in the tribe were under fifty, but there were a few who were old enough to remember.

Those elders listened out of a deep respect for the hardships people had faced then, and the others, including little Corrine, listened with great curiosity.

"During that time, many families were ripped apart or lived life in fear, or both. There were a few larger communities that had perfected their ways of life and created safety for their people, but not many. It was from one of those places that a man named 'Ezekiel' came.

"Ezekiel—you might better recognize him as 'the Founder'— traveled all over Irth in search of humans who hadn't been tainted by the Madness. His goal was to find a way to stop it, but he knew he could never manage that feat on his own. If he were to be successful, he would need help. He would need people he could trust and turn to for support.

"Someone like you?" Corrine asked.

The Chieftain smiled, enjoying her enthusiasm for his history lesson. He nodded. "Yes, but that comes later. Right now, I want you to learn where it all began. And our life now, in many ways, came about because of Ezekiel. Without him, I never would have found my way here."

Corrine smiled and nodded, settling back down quietly.

The Chieftain took her silence as his cue and continued, "In Ezekiel's journeys, he came across a small group of people who clung to the hope they could find happiness in a world of darkness. Those people were starving and injured, and some were at death's door, but they still held on. It was this fight in them that drew Ezekiel to them. Their will to carry on was exactly what he needed. If humanity were to survive, he would need that kind of inner strength to help him save it.

"In that time, things were very different. Magic hadn't yet manifested in humans, though other creatures had certainly been touched by something: magic, a curse—no one could be certain. Just waking up every day was a risk, and people could only hope a miracle would come along to save them. Unfortunately, that hope had quickly faded in most of us. Even I had begun to lose my way.

"It seemed like the world was doomed to fail against such a powerful darkness, but Ezekiel stumbled upon a group who believed in the Matriarch and believed she would once again find them, that she would come back for them. Within a very short period of time, he grew close to those people as he helped mend the ones who could be saved and bury the ones who couldn't, and they began to trust him. They saw him as an outside strength they could lean on, and they became even stronger."

The Chieftain prepared himself for the next part, Zoe pausing in her images of the middle-aged man scouring the lands for reliable people he might turn to. He knew the next bit would come as a shock to some, given how things had changed so drastically over the years—and how they had ended.

He cleared his throat again before continuing, "Among his new people, there were two he clung to most. One was a young boy of only twelve named Adrien, who had a pure heart and a willingness to help Ezekiel no matter what the task. The older man felt responsible for the orphaned boy, and soon began to treat him like his own.

"The other person he came to lean on was a *wildly* handsome and strong young man in his early twenties named Alexander." Everyone laughed as he said his own name, including Corrine. He looked at Arryn, but she only smiled knowingly at him, shaking her head.

She had to know that was coming...

"Before that time, I knew *very* little about planting or growing so much as a flower, let alone what we do now. Even when Ezekiel came, I was only just learning. I wasn't a farmer by trade, but had quickly picked up a talent for it once safe farmland and educated farmers became scarce. I had no other choice. I'd worked on farms, so I knew more than the average person, though it still wasn't much. I took that burden onto myself, and within only a short time, I learned how to grow almost anything, and did so to feed the people. Alaric and his brother Jerick helped me most."

Arryn shifted where she sat, catching the Chieftain's attention. "You knew Adrien from that young an age? I knew the three of you were involved with the Founder together, but I didn't know you knew one another even that far back."

The Chieftain nodded. "He was only about five or six when a small group wandered into our area. We didn't have many people, but they had even less. His parents had been killed, and friends of theirs had taken him with them. We accepted them and helped them. He was a strong-willed and kind young man, even at six. I liked him very much, and he assisted me often. When Ezekiel arrived, and the boy chose to cling to him, I wasn't surprised at all."

Arryn snorted. "Seems he craved power even then, attaching himself to the stronger men in the area in hopes of learning and growing."

The Chieftain smiled. "What you just described is exactly what any child does. It's natural. It's how they grow. To deny them a figure like that is to stunt their growth and limit their true potential. It's only because you know how that child turned out as an adult that you second-guess his motives. Trust me—I know, because I did the *exact* same thing. For many years I wondered if I, or even Ezekiel, had led him down that path."

She nodded, understanding his words. "That makes sense, I suppose. I guess I clung to you and Elysia. I still do. But if it wasn't lust for power that drove him early on, what was it?"

The Chieftain gave a sad smile, his eyes briefly drifting to the flames. "Fear." He paused. That word resonated with everyone there, most of all Corrine. "Fear, especially at a young age, makes people crave power. If they're strong, nothing can harm them. But then, how much is enough? Soon, it becomes an obsession.

"Arryn, I allowed you to come here because I knew that if you were left to grow up in Arcadia, terrified for your life, you would start obsessing over power. I had no idea what to look for in Adrien, but I sure as hell learned later. That's why young Corrine is with us now. We need to teach her, as we taught you, how to be strong without letting fear be a motivator. Power is intoxicating and addicting."

The young mystic to his right seemed just as invested in his response as Arryn and Corrine had been. The few children in attendance seem enraptured with his story, their parents hugging them tightly as he continued.

"Now, where was I?" He paused, looking at the stars for a moment before smiling. "Ah, yes. Before long Ezekiel decided he couldn't wait any longer to stop the Madness. He knew it would close in on all of us soon—as it always had—and would force us to uproot and begin again. I honestly can't tell you how many times we'd been forced to flee. But when he stood in front of us that day, we knew that time would be the last.

"He came to us early that morning, just after the sun began to show over the horizon. He said, 'How many times will you move? How many times *can* you move before there isn't a plot of land left that's safe?' That stopped us, forced us to think, but then he asked, 'How will you feed your children when you can't even guarantee you will survive the night?'"

He shook his head, thinking back on that day. "His words moved me. I was the first to stand, knowing that if the Madness weren't ended soon there would be nothing left worth saving. What many of you don't know—in fact most of you don't know —is that my late wife, Audrey, and I had a child. She was the light of my life, but was taken from us, killed by one of the Mad. The only thing that kept Audrey and me from giving in and allowing death to find us, too, was knowing she wouldn't have wanted us to live that way.

"She had asked us for a little brother or sister, something we didn't feel comfortable giving her because life was terrifying enough with one child. It was her love for family that reminded us of ours and kept us going. It was my *future* family I sought to save. It was *every* future family. Audrey and I believed children were a gift, and we always took great care to teach all children in our charge kindness, respect, and strength—both physical and emotional."

Elysia reached over and grabbed her father's hand, giving it a squeeze. She had known she had once had a big sister, but she didn't know much about her. Neither the Chieftain nor her mother ever spoke of her. Even after they succeeded in stopping the Madness, the loss was still too painful to think about.

"Without hesitation, after Ezekiel finished speaking I stood and said, 'I will join you. The thought that I might never again know what it's like to hold my own son or daughter in my arms is a fate worse than death. Family is all we have in this world, and if it's gone… Well, we have truly lost all hope then.' One by one, our people stood and offered themselves to Ezekiel's cause. We knew he was our best chance of fighting the Madness and surviving. We knew that even if *we* died in the process, *Ezekiel* would be successful, and our families would have hope."

"After that, we traveled to find who Ezekiel called the Oracle. We traveled for quite a long time and ended up finding others willing to join us. We happened upon yet another man with a strong will who brought determination to our cause."

Zoe smiled as she projected the image. "Selah," she said softly.

The Chieftain smiled and nodded. "Yes. Selah. Together, Ezekial, Saleh, Adrien, once he got older, and myself became the men our people turned to most. We were natural-born leaders. Men with good intentions, bravery, and a perpetual desire to succeed. As it turned out, those very qualities helped us shepherd our people through the hardest trials they would ever face to come out the other side *alive*. Alaric and Jerick were just behind us, my largest supporters, and I was grateful to have them—especially Alaric as we were very close.

"There will be time later to discuss the actual details of our long battle to end the Madness, but for now, we are skipping forward. Our battle had been won. The Madness had ended, though there would be a long road to recovery still. The consequences still lingered, leaving behind men and women who were no longer human, but hadn't fully succumbed to the effects.

"They became some kind of hybrid between human and beast. A taste for blood and violence, but with the capability to speak and think—even if it was scattered and most of it was insanity. You know them as the remnant and also lycanthropes. The remains of what once could have been the total annihilation of the human race.

"Once the Age of Madness was over, a new age began: Magic. And instead of moving on, Ezekiel decided he wanted to stay with us. We had become more than just acquaintances, friends, or allies in a fight. We were his people. *His family*, as we put it back then."

The Chieftain arched his back, popping it in several places before relaxing again and taking a long drink of his wine.

"As I said before, Ezekiel had grown up in an established community by the name of New Romanov. It was a place of peace and prosperity, even in the midst of the Madness. Everyone worked together for whatever they needed. We had tried to do the same thing before he came along, but things had progressed with the Madness to the point it had become almost impossible to do so. When he and Selah joined us, things changed.

"We traveled to a large valley with land fit for growing and building on, which we would eventually call the 'Arcadian Valley.' After we'd settled, Ezekiel began to teach us the magic he had learned that had allowed him to defeat the Madness. He didn't teach Adrien only physical magic, or me only nature, or Selah only mystical. He tried to teach us everything, but we each pursued what suited us best."

Zobig approached and flopped on the ground, creating a dust cloud. Curious, Corrine made her way to him and slowly reached out to touch him. His large paw was fast as it smacked her, knocking her on her backside.

She looked shocked for a moment, and the Chieftain reached over and helped her up.

"Don't worry about him, Corrine," Arryn said, pointedly looking at the bear, who was now rolling around on his back. "He's an old grump. He does that to *everyone*. Just look at him—he thinks he's hilarious."

The Chieftain laughed. "He *is* an old grump, but he's *my* old grump. You'll figure out soon how we met. Not tonight, but soon.

Just know he isn't being mean. Like Arryn said, he thinks it's funny. He trips even *me* sometimes. He's too fat and lazy to get up and do much else, so he has to entertain himself somehow."

The bear grumbled as he rolled back to his stomach. Though it took effort, he stood and wandered over to Corrine, nuzzling her with his head before going back to his spot, dropping to the ground again, and closing his eyes.

The Chieftain smiled. "Well, that was the nicest thing I've seen him do in a while. Anyway, back to the story. We are almost through with this portion, and next time we can get to the good stuff."

"I happen to think this *is* good stuff," Elysia said with a smile.

He quirked a brow at her. "And if I said this was the best part of the story?"

She smiled. "I'd tell you that you were full of it, old man."

He nodded. "See? You *did* inherit my sense of playfulness. You just choose to think you're better than me, like that ward you took in." He winked in Arryn's direction.

The Chieftain drank some more wine, finishing that cup before continuing, "During those first years, when everything was new, and we were trying to decide what direction the city should take, there were a great many arguments. Adrien was older now—just over twenty—and very opinionated. He and the Founder fought often, sometimes daily. The people began to grow tired of it.

"In those days, though we had *never* meant for them to, things had begun to change. Some turned to Selah with their troubles, others to me, many to the Founder, and quite a few to Adrien. Our society became less peaceful than we had hoped. It segregated, and the constant fighting only served to drive larger wedges. Eventually, many people came to me and told me they didn't want a life in a city. They wanted to live somewhere free and harmonious, somewhere that gave them the same feeling they had when using their magic. I gathered those people and we went west, toward the forest.

"Selah did the same with his people, and even Ezekiel departed, leaving Adrien in charge of Arcadia. The three of us still intended to continue working together for the good of *all* our peoples, though. Selah and I would need occasional resources, and we could provide harvested goods for the city. It was to be peaceful, even after the split, but that too changed. Adrien began to grow darker and darker, and eventually I was forced to close our borders. And *that* is where I will leave off for tonight, because that is where *our* story begins."

There were protests from the listeners, but the Chieftain said that it was time for the young ones to get to bed and everyone else to enjoy their night.

To Arryn's surprise, he hadn't wanted them to listen to him all night long. She wondered if it was because it was emotional for him to revisit those memories. Remembering how close he had once been to Adrien and the others that he had helped protect must have been hard, but talking about the daughter who had died must have been torture.

Hearing where everything began caused mixed emotions in Arryn. There had originally been so much hope and excitement. The plan had been to build a city—Arcadia—where people were safe and able to build families and create lives. They could practice magic and use it to make life easier and better.

Magic had never been meant to be a source of power. It was intended be a tool to enrich the environment and the mind. Mental magic was to be used to feel better empathy, and help loved ones through hardships. Physical magic could be used to build. Had it not been for physical magic, the buildings and roads of the new city would have taken much too long to build, and the Academy never would have been possible at all.

But nature magic… Nature magic resonated most with her. Had she been around back then, she would have chosen to be a druid. However, if things had gone the way the Founder had hoped, there would have been no reason to choose.

Like the others, she believed nature magic had a purpose—to heal the sick and create a world where children could grow old, and the old could die naturally instead of from fever or terrible diseases.

The three magics together would have created a utopian society. Everyone would have been useful and able to help their neighbors. Work would have been done easily, and families would have watched out for one another.

But the magic users had separated into their chosen disciplines. That segregation in and of itself hadn't been what caused the struggle, though. That had come about because of a single, bitter, power-hungry man who had wanted to be in control instead of being an equal.

Corrine yawned loudly, pulling Arryn from her thoughts. She smiled as the girl rubbed her eyes before leaning over and hugging Dante, who had once again come to lie next to her.

Arryn pulled her hand free of Cathillian's. "I need to get her to bed. She's exhausted."

"Need any help?" he asked, rubbing his own eyes.

"What, and give Nika and your mother even *more* reason to make jokes? No, I'm good. But thank you for offering." She smiled.

Arryn made her way to the Chieftain's chair and prepared to lift Corrine from the ground, but he beat her to it.

"Surely, I wasn't *that* boring, was I?" he asked the little girl.

She giggled, but it was weak, and her eyes were heavy. "No. I like hearing you tell stories, and Zoe made it fun." She gave another big yawn. "I've never seen anything like that before."

He clutched her tightly against his chest, smiling as he patted her back. "Well, you're home now, little one. You'll spend many nights around the fire listening—or telling stories of your own—though I can't promise the presence of a mystic. I think that's temporary."

Arryn smiled as she reached for the little girl. She had been through so much. She could barely imagine how hard life must have been for her before she journeyed to the Dark Forest.

Corrine immediately wrapped her arms around Arryn's neck, letting out a tiny sigh of contentment as she laid her head on Arryn's shoulder. When she felt the girl twisting her long hair around her finger, her breath caught in her throat.

Whenever her mother had carried her to bed as a child, that had always been her favorite thing to do. The older woman's hair had been so soft, and it had made her feel safe and comfortable just touching it.

Arryn squeezed her tighter, rubbing her back.

"We should set aside a space for her in the morning. Don't you think? Give her the official fresh start she deserves," the Chieftain said.

Arryn didn't even have to ask. She knew exactly what he meant. It was the same thing he had done for her when Elysia had brought her to the druids.

Arryn thought back on that time with fond memories. Arryn waking in a new place should have been terrifying, but that morning the Chieftain had taken her and Elysia with him to clear a portion of the village floor. Then he helped her plant seeds, and he and Elysia had germinated them and shaped the trunks they formed.

Within minutes, she watched as the trees bent, expanding in very delicate ways as the druids shaped their branches into a home. The leaves that formed the roof were so thick and tightly grown, not even the heaviest of rains could seep through.

The only difference was that Arryn had no idea back then

how to do even the simplest nature magic when she had arrived. This experience with Corrine would be much different.

Arryn smiled at the Chieftain and nodded. "I think that would be perfect for her."

CHAPTER TWO

Exhausted from the late night, Arryn had hoped to sleep just a bit longer that following morning, but that clearly wasn't the plan for the day.

She awoke to violent shaking, her eyes flying open as she sat bolt upright in her bed. Instead of danger, she saw hopeful grey-green eyes to her left and wise, old, and obviously-excited jade-green eyes from the foot of her bed.

"Is nothing sacred around here?" Arryn asked, flopping back down. "You're seventy. Why can't you be a crotchety old man who sleeps in too late?"

The Chieftain laughed. "You're only as old as you feel, my dear, and you guys keep me young. I might be the Chieftain, but I'm also the troublemaking community grandpa. Who else is going to teach them bright and early, and—"

Arryn smiled. "Yeah, teach the kids bad habits all day and get drunk with their parents all night!"

He pinched one of her exposed toes. "That's right! It's a huge responsibility to be this good-looking, adored, and popular with people of all ages."

Arryn lifted her head to shoot him an amused, but incredulous look. If she had been blindfolded, it would have been impossible to tell the Chieftain from his grandson. There was no question at all where Cathillian had gotten it from.

The old man winked at Corrine, who was just as excited as he was. Corrine's expression turned serious, though. "Please, Arryn? I'm so excited to have my own house! The Chieftain said we couldn't do it without you. Don't you want to do this with me? Don't you want to spend time with me?"

The girl puffed out her lip a little, and Arryn heard a slight snicker from the foot of her bed. Turning her gaze on the Chieftain, she caught the quick change in expression from amused to serious.

"Oh, Arryn. That's terrible. See what you did?" the Chieftain said.

She narrowed her eyes. "What is the matter with you? You told her to say that! What a rotten old man you are!"

"Yay!" Corrine cheered as Arryn climbed from her bed. "And don't be so hard on him. He said you'd be really sleepy, but we should wake you anyway."

Arryn laughed. "That isn't exactly a point in his favor, Corrine, but it's fine. I remember him telling me to do similar things to guilt Elysia into giving me what I wanted. Don't listen to him all the time, though. He'll get you in trouble and turn you into a spoiled little thing."

"What? I would never!" the Chieftain said, feigning shock.

Arryn stood and stretched. "You know, I'm really starting to think all of Cathillian's bad habits came from you. He does that *exact* same thing to me *all the time.*"

The Chieftain laughed. "Glad he learned something useful. Now, come on! You move too slow. Aren't you a morning person?"

Before Arryn could respond, the Chieftain turned toward the

door, with Corrine following closely. As they all stepped outside, the sun peeked through the canopy and blinded Arryn. It took her a moment to adjust.

The Chieftain sighed as he smiled. "The sun is certainly shining brightly this morning. Not a cloud in the sky! Now, off to find a good section of land for our newest druid."

"It's the Dark Forest," Elysia said as she passed. "It's *all* good land, Father." She turned to Arryn. "Good morning, dear. I'm sorry. I tried, but you know how he is."

Arryn smiled and shook her head. "No worries. Thanks for trying. Wanna come? You and I did this together. I feel like it should be a tradition."

Elysia thought for a moment before nodding. "I'd love to. After all, we'll probably be doing this again in another ten years for your children—by which I mean my grandchildren."

Arryn's eyes widened. "Well, I see Cathillian told you about the conversation he and I had. You seem to be finding that bit of information good and amusing."

Elysia shrugged. "The whole southern village has been waiting for this for years. Of course, I do! Anyway, after housing we'll have training, since you're up."

The four of them walked and talked as they searched for a piece of the forest within the village that felt like home for the young girl. As they spoke, Arryn became aware of just how different things were in the Terres Forest.

After picking her perfect spot next to a large bed of mixed flowers, Corrine said, "Okay! I'm ready. Do I get to cut down my own trees?"

Elysia gave her a smile, though it seemed to be more sympathetic than happy. "Here we don't kill the trees."

Corrine looked at her with total confusion. "Then how do you build your houses?"

The Chieftain extended his hand to Arryn, giving her the

seeds for the bamboo they would use. In the past, they had used trees with slightly thicker, but still flexible trunks instead of bamboo. That was what Arryn's house was made from. But they had begun using bamboo in recent years.

Arryn said. "Do you know how to plant seeds? Are the druids where you're from able to grow them?"

She nodded. "They can, but they don't very often. The forest is pretty there, but nothing like here. It's natural. I don't think they plant new things. They never taught me, though. I can call vines, but that's it. I learned how because I was always scared, and wanted to be high in the trees."

Arryn reached out with her free hand and gave Corrine's shoulder a squeeze. "All that's over now. And it's fine that no one taught you, because I will. Okay? We'll teach you the right way."

The girl smiled warmly before saying, "Thank you. This is the best gift I've ever had."

Unfortunately, Arryn believed that, but instead of focusing on the horrible life the young girl had led in her short years, she just returned Corrine's smile and handed her some of the seeds.

"Just follow my lead," she told her.

Arryn began crawling in a large square, dropping the seeds and pressing them into the dirt in tight lines. Corrine mimicked her actions.

Once the initial perimeter was sown, Arryn spread several throughout the middle.

"Okay," Arryn began, "when these grow, we will bend them to the shape we want. This bamboo will be the floor in your home. We will urge all the canes to bend and grow in a layer that will be woven together to create a strong foundation up off the ground, then another layer will grow over the top that will be completely flat."

As Arryn explained the plan, Corrine's eyes grew wide. "*That's* how you get your houses? How can you control the trees and bamboo like that? No one can do *anything* like that where I'm from. They can grow stuff, but that's about it."

"Once the floor is done, we will plant more seeds for the walls and roof. I know it doesn't make sense now, but trust me—it will soon."

Arryn smiled at her as she placed her hands flat on the ground on the opposite side from where Corrine knelt. The Chieftain knelt where the front of the home would be, and Elysia at the back.

Arryn, Elysia, and the Chieftain allowed their eyes to flash green, Corrine following shortly after. As the druids saw the neon-green color, they gasped.

"They look just like his," Elysia said to the girl, motioning to her father. "I didn't realize your eyes could turn green."

"The best shade, too," the Chieftain said with a wink in Corrine's direction. "You must be capable of using both light *and* dark magic. That's why your resting eyes are grey with hints of green, while your magical color is vibrant green. You have a lot of power in you, little one. Let's test it, shall we?"

She smiled and nodded, putting her hands flat on the ground in front of her like they had.

"Now, the magic where you come from isn't quite as different from ours as the dark druids' is. Otherwise, we would have quite a task on our hands," the Chieftain said as he leaned forward again.

He nodded to Arryn, and she began to explain the fundamentals of growing. The girl did her best to positively focus her power into the seeds, but failed several times.

"Watch me," Arryn said.

She leaned forward, focusing her will on the seeds to germinate them. A familiar heat began to fill her, flowing through her body and down through her hands.

The magic used to grow things wasn't entirely different from the magic that was used to heal, which was another thing Corrine hadn't been taught to do.

As Arryn called upon her magic, the Chieftain and Elysia called their magic as well. They pushed the magic slowly, so Corrine could help grow the seeds.

The girl's eyes continued to glow as she studied each of them closely, curiosity all over her expression, but finally she leaned forward and flattened her hands against the dirt again.

Arryn could feel the swell of energy within the girl, but it was tainted in a way she couldn't quite understand. It didn't feel quite like life, but it didn't feel so hopeless as death either.

It was a risk, but Arryn wanted to try something similar to what Amelia had done to test her strength not long ago when she had first arrived in Arcadia.

"Focus on where you came from. Focus on how terrible they made you feel. Remember what it was like to wake up every day in the trees, unsheltered from the rain, snow, or cold. Remember how bad their energy felt to you."

Corrine's eyes were locked on hers as she nodded her head, her dark grey curls bouncing a little as she did.

Arryn continued. "Now think about how you feel here. Focus on the good things that have happened in your short time here. You're about to have a place to call your own. You only need to grow it. Are you going to let those assholes in that forest hold you back?"

Corrine's eyes widened for a moment and she shook her head. "*No.*" It was only one word, but Arryn heard the conviction in it.

She closed her eyes and angled her face toward the ground in deep concentration. Arryn began to feel a shift in her magic, one that was angry, but somehow lightening.

Arryn and her Elders looked at one another as they felt the shift in the ground below Corrine, and Arryn smiled as the bamboo began to break through the soil.

Everyone pushed together then. Corrine grew the bamboo, and Arryn and the Elders bent and shaped it. The bamboo leaned over with little effort, each one weaving around the one next to it to create a floor solid enough to hold the weight of several people —or a heavy tiger, if Dante ever grew.

Once the two layers of floor had been created, the four of them planted more seeds and grew the walls, bending them at the top where they tightly wove them together again, only at an angle instead of flat.

The leaves grew thick and strong, ten times as many on each stalk as what grew naturally. This created a strong roof that could withstand any weather and would keep Corrine completely dry.

When it was finished, Arryn walked around the solid building in time to see the girl tip over a bit, her eyes heavy. She yawned and shook her head, trying to wake herself. "Why am I so sleepy?"

Arryn smiled. "You just used a lot of magic. *Good* magic. It'll get easier the more you practice, but right now you should probably go take a nap."

"You did well," the Chieftain said. "I never doubted you for a second. Arryn did, but not me."

Arryn snorted. "Old man, maybe *you* need a nap, too. Or a time-out. You're even more ridiculous this morning than usual."

"I second that," Elysia said with a laugh as she rounded the corner.

The Chieftain shook his head. "Honestly, I don't know how I raised such a stick-in-the-mud. Cathillian is the only one who gets it. Little Corrine, don't take after these two."

The girl laughed, and yawned again. Arryn reached out with her mind, and only a few moments later Snow arrived. She helped Corrine onto Snow's back before telling the big cat to take her back to her own house.

"Why can't I stay in mine?" Corrine asked, leaning over and snuggling into Snow's thick fur.

"Because it isn't ready yet. We still need to craft you a bed and get you some bedding. I know you're used to sleeping in the trees with nothing more than the clothes on your back, but that time is long gone. I want the first night you spend in your new home to be comfortable," Arryn said.

Corrine only managed a slow nod before her eyes shut.

"Okay, Snow," Arryn said. "She's already passed out. Make sure she gets into bed safely."

Once the tiger was on her way, Elysia gently smacked Arryn in the arm with the back of her hand. "You ready for some training?"

"Am I giving or taking the ass-beatings today?" Arryn asked.

Elysia smiled. "Oh, you'll be giving them. However, you're going to have to take one from me first. We have some new recruits. Gotta show 'em how it's done!"

"I'm not too excited to get in the pit with you this early, but I guarantee *they* don't want to be in there with *any* of us." She smiled deviously. "This should be fun."

As the sun rose high above the Terres Forest, Alaric's followers as well as Jerick's searched for the little girl the Dark Chieftain had met when he first arrived.

He and his people were supposed to head back early that morning. Everyone had been all set, but Jerick had stopped him.

"She was in the trees when we spoke," Jerick had said. "She's never been one of us, never understood most of the things we do or our way of life. She believes the world is inherently good. She is a foolish child, with beliefs that match Alexander's. If she went east—"

"Fuck!" Alaric had said. "You really think she would go to them? To warn them?"

Jerick gave a knowing smile. "A man wandered into our forest once. He was gathering berries for his family as they traveled and had gotten lost. They took from us—from *my* land. They knew we were here, and they didn't bother to ask. I had them killed, but that little bitch kicked and screamed trying to get past my men to them. She didn't understand that we have to protect our lands."

Alaric laughed. "Yeah, I wouldn't have stood for that. That would have been her last day on Irth. You're far more patient than I."

"That was what I said!" Jerick shook his head. "She's not one of us. She overheard us talking about you attacking the Dark Forest and me helping you, about smoking them out and killing them."

"Why the hell didn't you say anything earlier?" Alaric asked. "We could have done something about it *then*."

Jerick sighed. "Forgive me, Brother. I didn't really think about it. I knew she had problems, but deep down, I thought she would come around. Now that she's gone… Well, there's just no question as to what happened. You asked if she would have gone to the Dark Forest. I really think she would."

They sent their men and women into the forest to find any trace of her, but they heard nothing for several hours. When midday came, and the sun was at its peak, one of Jerick's men came in.

A tall man with pale grey skin, he had short hair, unlike most of the others. "Chieftain, we found something by the border."

Jerick rolled his eyes. "Well, don't wait around all day. What was it?"

"We found apple cores high in a tree. Most of us searched in the trees since that was where she spent most of her time. They found several apple cores on a branch high in an oak by the border. Another found a piece of her clothing that had ripped away when she crossed the border."

Alaric's eyes widened a bit. "Tell me that you didn't cross, too. Alexander sends his scouts very far out."

The warrior shook his head. "No. We spied the dirty cloth hanging on a broken branch in a tree just across the border. We knew not to approach, but it matched the last thing she was seen wearing, and wasn't far from the apple cores."

Alaric nodded. "Well, at least you were smart enough to stay put. While I get a particular enjoyment from fucking with Alexander, I don't want to risk anything I have planned."

"It might be too late for that already," Jerick said. "If she really has been gone since that night, she's already made it to them. She's capable of moving very quickly through the trees—even faster than we can go on foot on flat ground."

The men turned as Aeris approached. The younger man had worry on his face as he nodded to the short-haired warrior standing near Jerick.

"Chieftains," he said, regarding each man with respect. "I came to tell you what we found, but I see Keagan has beaten me to it. This is *not* something we can take lightly. The entire reason I left the Dark Forest was because they allowed outsiders to come in. They invited a young Arcadian into their borders to live with them. Not only that—she was considered *family* among the Elders. I couldn't let that go, not with all the betrayal the druids have seen from that bastard city."

Alaric turned more toward him. "What are you getting at, Aeris?"

"My sister stayed behind. She grew up with Arryn, and knew her well. She was also there when Arryn took her *Versuch*. If what Jenna said is true, the Arcadian grew into her power and is a force to be reckoned with. She *won't* go down easily.

"I knew Cathillian years ago, and Jenna trained with him before she left. He's just as strong. Alexander, Elysia, and Cathillian will be difficult, if not impossible, to beat with our low numbers."

Alaric sighed, not at all enjoying the sound of that. "He's right. The entire point of this plan was to weaken them; thin out their numbers so we could take them. We won't survive an assault on their territory with the number of able-bodied warriors I have."

Keagan, the short-haired warrior, seemed lost in thought for a moment before finally speaking. "If Corrine went to the Dark Forest and told them what you had planned, it's entirely possible Alexander will make a move on the Terres Forest first. He won't give you the time to go back south."

"If that's true, then our people are at risk," Jerick responded.

"Maybe that's a sign you should fight *with* me, Brother," Alaric said. "You know as well as I do that Alexander won't stop until we are all gone. Anything that threatens his precious forest meets a swift end."

Jerick thought that over for a moment before nodding. "It's been so long since we've seen one another. I'll be damned if I'll let him separate us again. We leave tonight. You'll have your army—and then you'll have your Dark Forest. We will share more land than any Chieftain ever has."

Aeris and Keagan smiled as their respective Chieftains began to discuss tactics.

"Shall we tell our people?" Aeris asked.

"Let Keagan do that. There's another task I want you to do for me," Alaric said.

"Yes. Anything, Chieftain," Aeris replied.

"You say this Arryn girl will be a problem?" the Dark Chieftain asked. Aeris nodded, and Alaric returned the gesture. "Good to know. I believe we have something to distract her with—don't you?"

Aeris' eyes widened a bit as a devious smile grew on his face. "Yes, we do. Once we get back to the south, I'll pay him a little visit."

With Aeris taking care of Arryn, all Alaric would have to

worry about was the others. He had a feeling they wouldn't be much of a problem once they lost their prized Arcadian druid.

That wasn't the first time Alaric had heard about the girl, though it was the first time he had heard about her having any kind of real capabilities. He personally knew it had been over ten years since she had seen her father.

It was about time for them to reunite...

CHAPTER THREE

Being back in her Capitol building office was strange for Amelia. She hadn't really been gone very long, but it had certainly felt like an eternity, with everything that had happened.

Everyone was attempting to return to their normal lives, but the confusion, the remaining fear, and sadness still permeated the air. Amelia knew it would be quite some time before all of it was gone, but that was why she had begun to make big changes.

Planning for a city council had already brightened spirits. Just knowing it was being formed was comforting to the citizens. No longer would a single person call all the shots. People would have a place to go where they could voice their concerns and even vote for change.

It was the only thing Amelia could think of that would give them the sense that they were free and in control of their own lives. Laws and rules had to be followed, but they had choices—something they had never really had before.

The first thing on her to-do list for the day was, "Speak with Elon." Not only had he helped her escape the city, he had assisted in the final battle against Scarlett and the remnant with his designs. And after the battle, he had stuck around.

He could have fled, but had instead chosen to stay. It was a decision she respected. She had already decided to pardon him for his actions during the battle against Adrien, but hadn't yet had the time to sit down and speak to him.

That was a problem she planned to correct that very day.

Though Marie had been promoted to Chancellor, she still acted as Governor Amelia's assistant until she could move into what had once been Adrien's office. A lot of work had to be done before that could happen.

First, the basement would need to be completely cleaned out, repainted, and repurposed. Talia had killed at least one student down there that they knew of, but she imagined more had fallen victim. It was horrifying to think about.

The office itself also needed extensive repairs. One entire wall had been blown out when Arryn had left to find evidence of Talia's being related to Adrien. She had found it, lost it, and found it again when Talia had taken her to the Frozen North and dumped her there to die.

Arryn had attacked Talia to get the letter Adrien had written to his daughter, and had planned to use it to prove her own innocence. She'd had no idea she would stumble upon something even more important—a birth certificate given to her by Talia's own mother, that had been signed by Adrien himself.

Amelia was now in possession of both of those valuable pieces of parchment, Arryn having given them to her before returning to the Dark Forest. They had been one more thing that had helped Amelia take back the control she needed to get things back to normal in Arcadia.

There was a knock at the door, which brought a smile to her face. It had been a long road, but she believed Elon was ready.

Amelia crossed her office, taking notice of the large blood stain that had sunk deep into the wood, as she still did every time she walked past it. It would have been easy to replace the boards, and she planned to do so as soon as possible, but for the time being she didn't mind at all. Marie's office was more important.

She opened the door and smiled again when she saw Marie and Elon standing there. "Your guest of honor has arrived," Marie said with a wink before heading back to her desk.

"Good morning," Amelia said, shifting slightly and extending her arm to invite him inside.

"Good morning," Elon responded, and he made his way over to the chairs in front of her desk, though he didn't sit.

"It's okay," she said. "You can take a seat. I'd like this to be comfortable."

He eyed her suspiciously as he sat. "You should know that Waylon and I have been working to improve the blast radius on those magitech mines. We are trying to get them a few feet wider. Once we figure out if it can be done without compromising the number of blasts that can be fired without overheating, we can start production again. Whether it can or it can't, we plan to start soon."

She smiled and nodded. "Thank you for the update. I really do appreciate it. In fact, I appreciate that work more than you know. It helped save the city. If we hadn't had those and Cathillian hadn't forced me into using them when we did, we could have been overrun."

Elon smiled. "Like we weren't with the druids and their trees?"

She laughed. "Yes, well, that was necessary. Plus, with a little work, those trees will make great lumber for rebuilding. So, while they tore up the street, they gave us something much better. The road won't be hard to fix at all."

Amelia reached for the pitcher on her desk and poured a glass of water for Elon before doing the same for herself.

"Speaking of rocky roads..." She sighed. "I know the one you've traveled has been hard for you. With Gregory, with the loss of everything you had—with all of it. It hasn't been easy."

"I think we both agree that I deserved what I got. My ignorance and blindness were no excuse. I should have understood when my actions caused Elayne's death. She didn't deserve that, and Arryn didn't deserve to lose her mother. Or her father, though she might still find him."

"I don't want to rub salt into old wounds, but I agree. You *did* deserve what you've gotten; maybe even more. But you have also gone to great lengths to fix what you did, as far as the city is concerned. I've said it before—I have no power to pardon you on Gregory's behalf, but I *can* on the behalf of the city," she told him, sliding a letter across the desk.

He watched the piece of parchment move toward him with confusion, and Amelia reached out, opening her senses to him. She could feel the fight inside him. Part of him wanted to reach for it, believing it was his salvation. The other part of him wanted to stay far away, not yet believing he had earned it.

"Your work doesn't have to end here, you know. When I give you this, it doesn't mean that you're done. It means that as far as I am concerned, you have repaired the damage you caused. If you don't feel you have, then why not keep working? You could stay here and continue to find ways to protect the city and better our weapons. You could also travel and find Gregory, maybe help people along the way. There is a lot you can do to continue on your journey to self-redemption."

Slowly, Elon reached for the piece of parchment and read it. It was a full pardon, written and signed by Amelia, stating that he had gone above and beyond to fix the mistakes he had made not only in the Battle for Arcadia, but even in earlier days.

She felt a wave of emotion as his eyes filled with tears. She looked down at her desk for a moment, and her eyes flashed white. Her mind wandered, brushing his and seeing his most intimate worries.

Elon feared seeing Gregory again. He feared telling him what he had done, and having his son not believe him. Most of all, he feared allowing himself to believe he truly was worthy of what Amelia offered, only to discover that he was wrong when Gregory found him.

Amelia wanted to comfort him. She had never done it before, but she had seen Julianne and some of the mystics in the Temple change the emotions of their target.

Amelia focused on her deep desire for him to be calm and content and pushed, trying to imagine it traveling outside herself and into him. At first his brows furrowed, but then they relaxed as he sighed and wiped his tears away.

"Thank you, Amelia," he said. "I'm grateful for the level of confidence you have in me. I don't yet know what I'll do, but having your support means more than you'll ever understand."

She nodded and offered a smile. "You're welcome. Let me know what you decide. I'll do my best to help with whatever it is."

Taking one last look at the parchment, Elon stood and reached across the desk. Amelia took his hand and shook it before walking him to the door.

Just before he left, he said, "Waylon took on another apprentice. Apparently, he's had one for quite some time. If I *do* leave, trust him. Waylon is a good man and can be trusted. The kid seems to be good, too, but I'm sure you'd be able to judge that better than I. The two of them will really make a difference with your new magitech mines."

With that, he turned to leave, and Amelia wondered exactly what would come next in his journey.

CHAPTER FOUR

Training had gone well, and it was time for a break in the day. Lunch was definitely in order, not only for her, but for all the warriors. They were exhausted, and the younger newcomers' training would only get harder.

It was Arryn's turn to get lunch, and she decided to take Corrine with her. It would be a good opportunity to see how she acted with forest creatures and what—if anything—she had been taught about the importance of hunting and the respect that must be shown along the way.

When she returned from the pit, she found Corrine with the Chieftain and the other children. They were gathered around a watermelon patch, and he was showing them how to pick the very best one.

"Arryn!" Corrine called excitedly as Arryn made her way over.

"Well, hello to you, too! Seems you had a good nap. How are you feeling?" she asked.

"I'm okay. We're about to have some watermelon! I've never had it. Is it good?"

Arryn looked at her with wide eyes. "You've never had watermelon?"

Corrine shook her head in response.

"Oh, hell. Well, you're going to love it! But that'll have to wait just a little bit longer, since I'd like you to help me with something. Is that okay?"

Corrine looked at the other kids, who had picked out a watermelon almost as big as Snow's head. "How long?"

Arryn laughed. "Not long at all. I'm taking you hunting. That watermelon is for the warriors' lunch. We spend the day training, and all the physical work really makes us hungry. So, the young children pick the vegetables and fruits and the older kids help prepare them while the warriors go hunting. It's my turn, and I wanted to take you with me. I'm one of the best hunters we have, so I promise it won't take long."

That seemed to satisfy the girl, and her eyes lit up as she ran to tell the other kids she would be back soon. Another little girl, Nayobi, gave Corrine a hug before waving at Arryn.

"Okay, I'm ready!" Corrine chirped as she skipped back.

A few seconds later, Snow arrived, and knelt for them to climb on. Then they were off, Snow running for the border. It took several minutes, but when they got there Arryn dismounted and placed her hands on the ground at its base.

Feeling her magic swell around her, she pushed it toward the barrier, urging the wall of thorns, vines, small trees, and various other plants to separate. The wall was now well over ten feet thick, having been reinforced by order of the Chieftain after several attempts—including a successful one—by the dark druids to enter.

Once the wall had opened, Arryn motioned for Snow to walk through before her, so she could close it after they had passed.

"What are we hunting for?" Corrine asked.

"Deer. They are in abundance here, and we can find them easily while not bothering their numbers. Did you hunt where you came from?" Arryn asked.

Corrine nodded. "I hunted for myself. Kids don't usually do it, but I kinda had to."

Arryn cleared her throat and nodded, trying to focus on the land ahead of her. "Okay, then. Well, let's see what you've got."

The girl seemed excited for the challenge, clapping her hands once before rubbing them together. She put them out in front of her, and her grey-green eyes flashed bright.

Arryn could feel the swell of magic as Corrine searched the immediate area for animals. She was surprised at the distance she could reach, but it wasn't anything near what one of the children her age in the villages could do. It showed just how strong she was, but if she'd had any training, she would have been capable of so much more.

It wasn't long before a large buck responded to her call. He leapt into their field of vision before cautiously approaching.

"Good!" Arryn said. "You're doing great."

Arryn was about to give her new instructions when she felt the magic begin to twist and become something much darker and colder. The buck cried out as he charged forward, his movements jerky and forced.

He stopped hard, hooves sliding across the ground for a few feet before he cried out again. Arryn was shocked, distracted by what she was seeing and feeling. As the buck lowered his head, prepared to fight the magic and charge again, Arryn snapped out of her daze.

"Corrine!" she shouted. "Stop, stop, *stop*! You're hurting him!"

The girl's eyes widened as she looked up at Arryn with confusion and what appeared to be an added mix of fear and worry.

"What?" she asked, her voice quivering a bit.

Arryn heard the rapid footfalls as the buck charged and realized that when she had told Corrine to stop the girl had done exactly that. She'd dropped her hold entirely. The buck was now enraged, and coming straight for them.

Arryn shoved Corrine out of the way and tried her best to get clear as well, but it was too late. As she jumped to the side, his long antler pierced the left side of her soft belly before throwing her off to the side.

Corrine screamed as Arryn hit the ground hard, then rolled farther out of the way, and climbed to her feet with tears streaming down her face. A loud roar battered their ears as an incredibly pissed-off Snow ran straight for the buck.

"No!" Arryn shouted at both Corrine and Snow. "Stay there! Snow, protect her."

The girl stopped hard, swallowing as she silently nodded. Snow growled low as she stood between the girl and the buck.

Arryn could hear the large deer snorting as he lowered his head again, preparing to gore Corrine this time. She didn't want him to be killed, not after he had been subjected to such pain and fear. If she could manage it, she would call on her magic to soothe him—if she could keep Snow from ripping him to shreds for hurting her and threatening the girl.

Groaning, Arryn clutched her side and gritted her teeth as she climbed to her feet with the aid of a small tree. "Hey!" she shouted, getting the buck's attention.

"Arryn, no!" Corrine screamed, her voice catching in her throat.

Taking a deep breath, Arryn stepped away from the young tree she had used to pull herself up, and her eyes flashed green as the buck ran for her again. She extended her hand in front of her as she pushed with all she had.

"Stop," she whispered. "Just… stop."

The buck hesitated for a moment before responding, but managed to stop hard only a few feet in front of her. Had her magic not taken hold as fast or as strongly as it had, she would have been wounded again—or dead.

Arryn heard Corrine's deep intake of breath but ignored it as she slowly approached the deer, limping with every step.

When she reached him, she placed her hand against his jaw,

still pushing her power to him. "Shh… Easy, boy," she began, wincing as pain radiated through her. "She's still very young, and just learning. She didn't mean to hurt you. She stopped when I told her to. You're no longer in pain. You're fine."

The buck brought his nose to her face, sniffing her a few times before sniffing at her side where he had injured her. She felt a wave of sadness from him when he realized what he had done to her in his rage.

"Shh… Don't worry about that," she whispered, stroking his neck. "It's all okay. I'll heal. You should go now. You're free."

Arryn lowered her hand and stumbled back a few steps, releasing him from her hold. He stood there, staring at her for several moments before turning and running away. Once it was obvious they were out of danger, Arryn fell to her knees, grinding her teeth again as she winced in pain.

Corrine ran across the space between them, coming to a quick stop in front of her. "Arryn," she whimpered, tears pouring down her face. "I'm so sorry. I was just doing what I always do. It's all I know how to do. Please forgive me! Don't send me back there, please!"

Without saying a word—because she was unable to speak right then—Arryn grabbed the girl's hand and placed it on her open wound. Taking a couple of deep breaths, Arryn croaked, "Heal it."

Corrine shook her head, wiping her tears with her free hand. "I can't. I don't know how."

"You're scared… yes?" Arryn said between breaths.

Corrine nodded in response, some of her tight curls that had come loose bouncing around her beautiful face. "I don't want to lose you."

"Call your magic."

Corrine's eyes flashed bright green again as she looked at Arryn in confusion.

"Your emotions are your greatest weapon, not weakness. The

magic you used to grow the bamboo with us…" Arryn groaned deep in her throat as more pain took her. "Call it."

Corrine once again did as she was told, and Arryn felt the life-bringing magic surrounding her.

"Now push it through your hand into me. All the fear and worry you feel right now, push it out of you and into me."

Arryn reached out and wiped Corrine's face as her eyes closed tightly in concentration. It took several excruciating moments, but Arryn finally felt the heat blooming where the girl's hand touched her skin. Soon, the pain disappeared altogether.

Arryn took a deep breath and gently pulled away, inspecting Corrine's work. The wound was jagged, and there was a large scar, but it was healed. Arryn knew it would continue to heal and eventually disappear completely, even if she didn't use magic on it. It would just take a couple days longer.

That was the power of being a druid—your injuries healed, even without being forced. It was the only reason she had survived Scarlett and Talia bleeding her out on the way to the Frozen North.

"I'm sorry," Corrine said again. "I didn't—"

Arryn reached out and pulled the girl into a hug, and kissed the top of her head. "You're not going anywhere. You didn't hurt me. I should have reacted sooner. I was… Well, to be honest, I was just very shocked."

Pulling back, Arryn smoothed Corrine's hair out of her face before shifting into a more comfortable position.

"I didn't realize I was hurting him more than a normal hunter would. Not until you told me." Corrine looked toward the ground, disappointment on her face.

"You did great calling him to you—that was perfect. Every-thing after that was wrong, but that's okay. You didn't hurt him permanently, and I soothed him. We're going to teach you the right way. The thing is, we aren't *normal* hunters. When we hunt, the animal never feels even the tiniest bit of pain."

Corrine's eyes widened as she turned back to Arryn. "You can do that?"

Arryn nodded. "And so can you."

"How did you do that? You forced him to do what you wanted, but he didn't seem to be in pain."

"From what I know about dark druid magic, when they create a familiar or call an animal, they don't do it like we do at all. We push our magic and create a bridge between us and the animal. We make it feel safe and ask it to come to us."

The girl looked uncomfortable. "Then what do *we* do?"

"*They* use their power to overwhelm the animal. They push so much influence toward it that the magic literally beats it into submission. Their magic takes over its brain and its body, and it's incredibly painful. It's not much different from what a mystic can do to a human. A dark druid's familiar isn't loyal out of love like Snow, Dante, and I share. It's loyal out of debilitating fear."

Corrine's eyes widened again, her lips parting slightly as the weight of her heritage settled on her.

"But you don't have to worry about that, now do you? You're not one of them, right?" Arryn asked.

Hope filled the girl's face as she sat up straighter and shook her head. "No. I never have been."

Arryn nodded. "Exactly. You learned their way because that's what you saw—you didn't have a choice. You didn't *choose* the people you learned from. If you had been in the same situation here with us—which never would have happened—but if you lived in the trees here, you would have picked up how to properly call an animal and probably how to heal or grow food. So, don't focus on *you*. This isn't your fault, it's *theirs*. They failed you. You didn't fail. Understand?"

She nodded. "I understand." There was a pause before she said, "Arryn, I want to learn to be like you. I want to use good magic. You're so strong, and you took an antler to the belly for me. No one has ever cared so much about me. Just tell me what to do, and I'll do it!"

Arryn smiled. "Good. I'm glad to hear it. Trust me, you won't be disappointed. First things first… We need to get some food to the warriors, or we're both gonna be in trouble. I'm too weak to call anything else, and I'm betting you are, too. How about we let Snow take this one?"

Corrine smiled and nodded. "I think that's a good idea. I'm kinda sleepy again."

"That'll happen. You have some strength in areas, but healing and growing take the most out of you. Tomorrow, we'll start bright and early. It'll have to be, because I have training at sunrise, so be ready," Arryn said.

"I will. What are we gonna do?" Corrine asked as she climbed to her feet, extending her little hand to help Arryn up.

Arryn took it, but used her own strength to keep from pulling the girl over. "I'm going to teach you how to call animals and communicate with them. You have no idea just how useful it can be. I'm not a native here, as you can probably tell by my rounded ears, but I'm the best at talking to animals. In fact, do you wanna do something really funny with me? It's my *favorite* thing in the world to do, and I haven't done it in a super long time."

Corrine seemed excited. "Yeah! What is it?"

Arryn gave a devious laugh. "Well, first we'll send Snow out, then you and I are going to hunt down a squirrel and have him send Cathillian a message."

CHAPTER FIVE

The Chieftain settled into his favorite chair at the firepit with his dual mugs of wine. He took a sip of the sweeter one and set it down by his feet. People had begun to gather when Zobig laid down next to him.

"Good evening, Zo," he said. "You gonna be nice tonight, or do you have plans to growl at the new baby?"

The bear grumbled before rubbing his head against the Chieftain's leg.

Smiling, Alexander reached down and scratched through his thick fur. "Good boy."

Arryn sat in her regular place, while Corrine once again picked the spot at his side.

"I hear you two had quite an adventure today," he said.

"It was pretty terrible," Corrine replied as she played with a small stick on the ground.

"It was a learning experience, dear," the Chieftain said. "You have to start somewhere. Besides, it sounds to me like you will be getting special training from here on out from one of our best. With a teacher like Arryn, you can't go wrong. She was a slow learner, so she understands better than most."

"Hey!" Arryn said.

He laughed. "What? You really were, but we loved you all the same."

"Yeah," Cathillian said, sitting next to them. "*Very* slow. He's being generous."

Corrine laughed as Arryn shot him a look that would possibly have killed a lesser man.

"By the way," Cathillian said, "I got your message. Funny."

Arryn looked at Corrine and winked. "You're welcome."

"What's this?" the Chieftain asked.

"Nothing," Arryn told him with a big smile.

"Yeah, nothing—except my room was *filled* with acorns and nuts. I don't mean there were a few. I mean there were three to four inches at least of nuts all over the floor, and my bed was full. They had to have been at it *all* day. I caught a damn squirrel in there stuffing them in my sheets and another one stuffing them in my pillow."

Arryn laughed so hard that she actually tipped off the edge of the log she was sitting on and fell to the ground.

"*Shit,*" she said, wiping tears from her eyes as she tried to catch her breath. "They went above and beyond."

"Yeah. The note left on top of the nuts piled on the bed was pretty *precious,* too," he said, mock annoyance in his voice.

"Read it!" Arryn said, snorting before bursting into laughter again as she bounced and clapped her hands in exaggerated excitement like a child. "*Please* read it."

The Chieftain nodded, and he laughed as well. "Yes, Grandson. Please do."

"Gladly! You'll see just how big an asshole she is." Cathillian pulled a small piece of parchment from his pocket and unfolded it before exaggeratedly clearing his throat and straightening his posture. "Dearest Cathillian, Chippy the Chipmunk asked me to let you know his nuts are still bigger than yours. Signed, Nutty the Squirrel."

Arryn screamed as she laughed, even slapping her knee. "*Damn!* That Chippy is a real—"

"Don't say it," Cathillian interrupted.

"*Nutcracker,*" Arryn croaked before exploding again, everyone else joining her.

"Mmhmm," he groaned. "How inappropriate for you to teach the young and impressionable Corrine such vulgarity."

Arryn looked at him incredulously, a smile still on her face. "First of all, *I* wrote the note. Secondly, it was *excellent* practice. She and I spoke to several friendly neighborhood squirrels, so it was a lesson in how to communicate with animals. She *also* learned about having a great sense of humor. I think she's taken to it."

Cathillian threw his hands in the air. "Great! Then I'll now get to enjoy the *two* of you teasing me with woodland creatures and notes."

More people filled the area, Zoe and Elysia among them. "Good evening, Chieftain," the mystic said with a smile.

She came over to stand next to him, preparing for the next part of his grand story. Only this time, she planned to do much more. The Chieftain had told her he would be recounting more details this time instead of hitting only the highlights of everything that had led them to retreat into the Forest as he had the night before.

The first time, Zoe had used a series of fast-moving images that had entertained, but didn't have as much detail as she liked, because the story had been told quickly. She had assumed he wasn't as good a storyteller as the mystics from the Temple, but she had realized he'd had to get through several years of backstory to reach to what he needed to say.

Tonight would be much different, and both she and the Chieftain were excited. The images would be much more complex and fluid as she connected to the memories. They would play out as if everyone were there.

"Good evening, Zoe," the Chieftain said. "I'm glad you could join us. I think the show tonight will be even more fun for everyone."

She smiled and nodded. "I think so, too. Shall we get started? Everyone is here."

The Chieftain nodded before picking his sweet wine up and taking a long drink. "Thanks to everyone for coming! Tonight... we head into the Dark Forest."

THE WESTERN FOREST was brand new for many of Alexander's tribe. Some of them had known only their very small community for most of their lives. Those who were old enough to have moved several times after having found safety for a time knew the peace that simply being in the forest could bring, let alone living in one.

It took several days to get to their destination. There were only a few horses for all of them, so everyone walked part of the time.

There weren't many in their group at the beginning, but as they passed other small groups on the way to the Forest their numbers increased. Alexander was sure those numbers would grow even more as time went on and Adrien became more terrifying.

Upon first look, this forest was no different than any other. There were trees all around, some of them having suffered damage from lightning, wildlife, or insect populations. The vegetation was overgrown in many places, with thorns and other hazardous plants growing out of control.

When Alexander had been around plants before, he hadn't known about them, but now he could sense things. He somehow knew how they grew and what they were capable of.

As they traveled, he did his best to point out what plants were okay to touch, and which were deadly or would make them sick. He made a mental note to destroy the harmful ones, so the forest would be less hazardous for the children as well as the animals that lived there.

They had walked for nearly half a day inside the Forest before they came across a patch of land that was more overgrown than the rest. The vegetation was the same dark green they had seen the whole way there, but he could feel something else. This land was different.

It felt like home.

"This is it, isn't it?" Audrey asked, a large smile on her face as she looked around.

He gazed at her face, lit by the sun shining through the trees and hitting her beautiful features, and he knew she felt the same thing he did.

Alexander nodded as he looked from her to the people behind them—his tribe. Some of them seemed to be just as taken with the area as he and his wife were. "I believe we've found our home," he told them.

"I've never seen anything like it," his best friend said.

Alexander nodded. "Alaric, my friend, with a little work I think this will be paradise. This could be the safe place we have all prayed about for our families."

Alaric shook his head, still looking around. "With a little work? This place is perfect just the way it is. It's beautiful!"

Alexander clapped a hand on his best friend's shoulder, pointing at various things around them. "There are many poisonous plants that need to be removed, so it'll be safe for the children. We'll need to clear land to build homes, but we should find a way to do it without destroying the Forest. There's no point in us moving here if we destroy what drew us to it in the first place."

"Alexander, you sound foolish. How can we build without cutting down trees? Is that even possible?" Alaric smiled and moved to the side, patting Alexander's shoulder in return. "But if you can figure it out, I suppose it wouldn't hurt to learn."

Audrey joined the two. "I think we both know he'll take that as a challenge."

"He always does," Alaric agreed.

Just then loud howls ripped through the area, bringing everyone to a *dead silence. Everyone looked at one another with fear on their faces, unsure how to proceed.*

"Were those wolves?" Audrey asked.

Alexander took a step forward, listening as another round of howls and growls echoed through the woods around them, and slowly shook his head. "No. Alaric, get the kids to safety."

"No. I can help you! Send her. It makes more sense." He narrowed his eyes at Alexander.

He wanted to have Alaric help him and send his wife with the children, but the truth was that his magic wasn't nearly as strong as Audrey's. Something big was coming, and she could help him the most. Alaric was much better suited to keeping the children safe.

"I know you want to help, my friend, but helping the children is helping me. I can't fight while worrying if they're okay. Please watch the children and make sure nothing happens to them," Alexander pleaded.

Giving Alaric no opportunity to protest further, Alexander grabbed his wife's hand and ran toward the threatening sounds. As they approached, they heard footsteps heading directly toward them.

"What is it?" she asked.

"I sense life, but that's as far as my knowledge goes. It doesn't feel like an animal or a human," he said, confusion obvious in his voice.

They stopped, and the footsteps closed in from all sides. The growls grew louder as the beasts approached. The first leapt over some tall brush, and their eyes widened in shock and terror as they realized what they faced.

The beast was tall, taller than Alexander. He had an elongated snout, and the face of a wolf. His shoulders and torso were those of a man, but broad with the musculature of an animal used to running through the woods. Its legs were thick, and an extra joint caused them to bend backward in the middle of what would be the shin on a human. The beast had massive claws on its humanoid hands and feet, but was covered in fur from head to toe.

Audrey took several deep breaths, fighting the urge to run. "What is that thing?"

"It's both man and beast, but neither," Alexander said quietly.

A roar sounded behind them, causing them to jump. Each turned their head enough to see three of the beasts leap out behind them while keeping an eye on the one ahead.

"Can we do this?"

Alexander nodded slowly, his hand reaching for Audrey's. "We have no choice. If we can't stop them, the others don't have enough magic to. The children will die."

His wife's eyes glowed as she stared at their enemy, and Alexander's turned bright fluorescent green as his magic responded. The first lycanthrope attacked and they both ran directly for it, each dropping to the ground and rolling in opposite directions just before the beast could grab them.

They rolled into a crouched position and thrust their arms out, one vine bursting from the ground in response to each and wrapping around the monster. Alexander swung his arm to the side, flinging the creature hard into a sturdy oak not far away. Its skull cracked against the thick trunk.

Alexander and Audrey stood up then, running for the next one while making as much noise as possible and feinting toward the others.

A large black lycanthrope turned toward them, alerting the grey one just next to him, and they both charged at Alexander and his wife. They tried to do the same thing as before, each rolling in opposite directions, but it didn't work this time.

As Audrey dove to the right, the grey beast went after her, slashing downward with his clawed hand and opening deep gashes across her chest and stomach. She cried out as she dropped to the ground, but pulled a knife from her belt and slammed it into his stomach. As he howled in pain and doubled over, she pulled the blade free and thrust it underneath his chin into his brain.

As he fell to the ground, she pulled the blade free, and called just enough magic to heal the potentially deadly wounds. Within a few seconds, they weren't completely gone, but they were no longer serious. She ran to help Alexander.

He dodged swipe after swipe from the massive claws, dropping to his knees and diving between the beast's legs. He rolled to his feet, then turned and thrust his blade into its back. Audrey slashed its throat as it fell to the ground.

Alexander wondered why the other two beasts hadn't attacked, and when he turned toward them he quickly discovered the reason.

Alaric, eyes glowing green and hands extended in front of him, stared at the last two as they screamed and howled in pain. Alexander could see that fatigue was rapidly overtaking him. Whatever magic he was using was dark—it felt cold, like death itself. Certainly nothing Ezekiel had taught them.

Alexander realized he had no idea what that magic was.

Alaric stumbled, bringing Alexander back to the situation at hand, and he rushed forward, driving his dagger into the throat of one as Audrey took care of the other. Within seconds both monsters were on the ground, quickly followed by Alaric.

Alexander rushed to his side, placing one arm around him and the other under his neck for support. "What the hell was that? It didn't feel like any nature magic I've ever seen."

Alaric smiled weakly. "Well, it's not like we've been at this for very long. I call it the 'death touch.' I don't know how it works or why I can do it, but I use it when I hunt. It keeps the animals from feeling pain if someone's shot isn't true."

He struggled to sit up, and Alexander assisted him. If it was true, that magic could actually be a good thing. Ezekiel had taught Alexander to heal, and he in turn had passed the knowledge to his people. He didn't know how to drain an animal's life, nor could he think of a reason one would want to.

And while his friend's explanation made sense—to end the suffering of a dying animal—something in his heart told him the man wasn't being completely honest.

Alexander heard crying and quick footsteps, drawing his gaze toward the sounds.

"Oh, goddess!" Audrey exclaimed, rushing toward a man and a woman carrying a small child.

Alexander stood and ran toward them, sensing that the child barely had any life left inside of him. "What happened?" he asked as he laid his hands on the child, his eyes glowing bright green as he pushed his magic through the boy.

The woman swallowed, her eyes briefly flickering to Alaric before turning back to Alexander. "Just after he left, a beast like those rushed out of the heavy brush and attacked us. I lost my father, and Caitlin lost her twin sister. They came for Jameson, too, but we managed to take them down."

"They? Them?" Alexander asked, watching as the boy's breathing became stronger. He gave a sigh of relief. "How many were there?"

The mother cried in happiness, pulling her son tighter against her chest and holding him as she sobbed. Again, her eyes wandered to Alaric, tears falling down her face. "I'm sorry. I can't shield him. I won't. He told us we were strong enough to protect ourselves, that there were more of us than there were of you. I know we far outnumbered the two of you, but he's next in line for strength of power after both of you. That was why you left him with us.

"Had he been there, we wouldn't have lost the two people, and my son wouldn't have nearly died. Yes, we killed those monsters, but we're all exhausted, and it took everything we had. Our magic is growing, but we aren't nearly as strong as he is, and not even close to either of you."

Alexander ran his fingers through the boy's hair. It was wet with blood, and it turned his stomach. It reminded him too much of the day he had lost his own child. He hadn't possessed any magic then, but he did now, and he thanked Bethany Anne for that gift and for allowing him to save young Jameson.

With anger in his eyes, he turned towards the man he had grown to trust, the man he had known for many years. "I told you to stay with them. Why did you leave? We had this."

Alaric stood on unsteady feet. "You would've died. You would've failed without me, and you know it."

Alexander shook his head, unable to believe the level of narcissism coming from his friend. Alaric had never seemed the type. "We might have, but it was just as likely that we would have survived. We were aware of the dangers, and knew how many we faced. Neither of us are tired, and we've used far more magic than anyone here. Well, except you. That death touch of yours is quite the drain, isn't it?"

Alaric snorted. "What's your point? Why am I the one being chastised here when I saved the lives of our almighty Chieftain and his beloved Audrey? Where would all these people be if you were dead?"

"My name is Alexander. Do not use a title I haven't earned to insult me. The point I was trying to make is that we used more magic than all of them, and we're fine. They're exhausted. It took everything they had to defend themselves, and two of them still died. Your power was better used protecting them, like I told you to do. As for what would've happened if we had lost our fight... Well, I suppose the people would've been left in your very capable hands then, now wouldn't they?"

Alaric's brows creased. "And what exactly is that supposed to mean?"

"Sweetheart," Audrey said softly, gently grabbing his hand. "He's been your friend for many years. Emotions are high right now. We lost two of our own. We saved the life of the child, and he saved our lives. If he hadn't, it's possible the child would've died. Don't argue. Let it go. Don't say something you'll regret later."

Alaric stared at Audrey for a moment before sighing. "She's right. It happened. We lost two people who deserve our respect. Right?"

Alexander admired his friend's ability to put the argument aside, but there was still something there. He had never questioned Alaric or his motives before, so he didn't understand why he would choose to do so right then, but there it was, in the pit of his stomach. A twisting feeling, trying to warn him.

Putting that aside, Alexander nodded. "You're absolutely right. Come, let us give them a proper sendoff, then we'll break ground on our new home. We came here for a purpose—to find peace. They didn't die in vain. They gave their lives to help us find it."

As he stood there, eying Alaric, the two of them calming down,

Alexander sensed something. It was new and blossoming. It was something he hadn't sensed before that moment, and he wondered if it was because of his heightened emotions. He wondered if his power was sensitive because of it.

He turned and looked to Audrey, smiling as he placed his hand flat on her lower abdomen. He could sense a completely separate life force thriving inside of her.

Her eyes widened as a cautious smile grew. "What is it?"

Alexander had to take a moment, wanting to be absolutely sure. Finally, he nodded. "It's our baby. The Matriarch has blessed us with another baby. A brand new life to bring into our new home."

THE CHIEFTAIN TOOK another long drink of his wine, taking a moment to reflect on the story he had just told and seen projected in front of him as if it were happening all over again.

Elysia smiled as she looked at her father, obviously enjoying the opportunity to hear about the moment they discovered her existence.

"With the pregnancy and with the deaths of our friends, everything calmed down for a while, but his lies never stayed dormant for long, and my suspicions grew all the time. I could sense the changes in him," the Chieftain said.

"You were friends for so long," Arryn said. "It must've been the nature magic that let you sense something different in him. Or maybe, having the extra power was what changed him. It seems like that was what happened to Adrien."

The Chieftain nodded. "Unfortunately, I think it was a mix of both. I still believe he was a good man before the power came along. I never would've thought nature magic could turn someone bad like that, but it did. And in case anyone is curious, as you all know, we *did* end up learning the death touch, but it was taught strictly as a way to end the suffering of any living thing that could not be healed, or for hunting."

He sighed, looking to the sky before lifting the stronger wine to his lips.

"Wrapping things up for the evening, that night we laid our friends to rest and celebrated the new life we were about to begin. The following day, we began anew, practicing our magic on the Forest. We raised new plants and strengthened the trees. Everything grew brighter, bigger, stronger. Soon, the canopy had become so thick we called this the Dark Forest.

"For weeks we camped out under the stars. And finally, after nearly a month, we learned how to grow our very first living home. It took a couple tries, but we succeeded, and I proved Alaric wrong. Next time, we'll pick up a little farther forward. Everyone enjoy your night."

With that, the Chieftain took his mugs and walked away, Zobig following closely. He knew he had cut things off rather abruptly, but he didn't want anyone to see just how hard it was for him to discuss not only his late wife, but also the man who had once been his best friend and was now his enemy.

CHAPTER SIX

Just as promised, it was very early when Arryn went to wake Corrine, but surprisingly the girl was already up. A small bird flew out her window as Arryn walked in.

"Well, good morning," she said with a smile as she sat on the edge of the new bed.

"Good morning! I'm ready to go," Corrine chirped, pulling her hair back as best as she could with a piece of leather.

Arryn motioned for her to sit, and she took the strap, helping Corrine fix her thick, kinky hair. She had been taking lessons on how to better fix the young girl's full, textured hair from Cassondra, one of the other druid warriors.

"I'm surprised to see you up so early after our late night," Arryn said.

"I didn't think I would be able to wake up on my own, so I asked a bird to come wake me when she woke up."

Arryn froze, a cautious smile spreading on her lips. "You asked a bird to wake you, and she did?"

Corrine nodded, testing her hair. "It took me a couple tries, but she finally understood me and said she would. I promised to bring her babies a big, fat worm."

Arryn laughed. "Well, we need to make sure to keep that promise. The last thing you wanna do is piss off a momma bird and get her chirping with the other moms out there."

Arryn made her way outside, Corrine close behind. "The idea for this morning was to teach you how to better communicate with animals, but it seems like yesterday's events with Nutty and his friends made a huge difference. Ha! Take *that*, Cathillian."

Corrine laughed. "You like him, don't you?"

Arryn's eyes widened. "Yeah, but I think that's a conversation for later. Much later." She exhaled, putting her hands on her hips as she looked around the dark village. "Wanna go to the pit? You haven't seen the *Versuch* pit yet."

"What's a verrr…"

Arryn laughed. "*Versuch*. It means 'trial.' When someone wants to leave the safety of our walls here in the Dark Forest, they have to take a test and pass it. There are three trials: magic, hand-to-hand combat, and weapons. You have to pass all three if you want to travel. It probably sounds like a loss of freedom to you, but it's how we know the person can take care of themselves outside. We want to know they'll be safe without the rest of us."

"Will I have to take the *Versuch*?" Corrine asked.

"Are you one of us?"

Corrine nodded. "Yes, I am."

Arryn gently pinched her arm. "Then I guess you'll have to take the *Versuch*! You have to be sixteen, though, so you're kinda stuck here for eight more years. You ready to go?"

The two walked toward the pit, Snow sleepily wandering up and ambling next to them. When they reached it, Nika was already there, lighting the torches and getting everything ready for training.

"Damn," Arryn said. "You got here early."

Nika smiled. "So did you. What are you doing here before dawn?"

Arryn nodded toward Corrine. "She hasn't seen the pit yet, so

I thought I'd show her." Pointing to Nika, she told Corrine, "She is one of the fiercest warriors we have. She might not look like much, but she damn near ripped my head off more than a few times."

Corrine's eyes widened. "When you train, you actually fight each other?"

Nika laughed. "Pain is the best motivator, young one. If ever you decide to go into training, you'll learn pain is your friend. When you feel it, you want to keep it from happening again. Whatever caused it, you'll learn not to allow that to happen again."

Arryn held up her hand. "I can vouch for that. I've had more broken noses than anyone here, I think."

Nika smiled. "Not everyone. If I'm to be honest, I think I had way more when I was your age."

"Why do you do that? Do all warriors fight that hard, or just the women? The men don't have to train so hard, right?" Corrine asked.

Arryn and Nika shared a knowing look. "Did someone tell you men are better fighters than women?" Nika asked.

Corrine nodded. "Women aren't allowed to be warriors where I'm from. They're healers, though it's nothing like I've seen the kids practice here."

Nika knelt, her eyes staring right into Corrine's. "Don't ever let anyone tell you that you can't do something. You are more than capable of kicking the ass of anyone you want to, whether they are a man or a woman. If it needs to be done, don't be afraid to do it."

"Yeah, emphasis on the 'man' part. She's mean."

Everyone turned to see Cathillian wandering up, rubbing his eyes.

"What are *you* doing here?" Arryn asked.

He snorted. "Who could sleep with all this racket going on? You guys talk *so* loud. And I think we have a new contender for the noisiest bird in the village. I thought Echo was the winner, but she and I both disagree with that now."

She looked at him incredulously. "We have been standing outside for two minutes, whiner."

He shrugged. "Anyway, Corrine, if you want to be a warrior, don't think about stuff like that. Here, women are just as dangerous as the men. Probably more. When someone sees a man, they assume he'll be powerful. A woman—not so much. That allows our women to take advantage of those weak-minded bastards and *really* get the upper hand. Not that they need it, but it's kind of funny to watch. I've had my ass handed to me *thoroughly* by Nika *and* Arryn, so don't let anyone tell you a woman can't kick ass."

Corrine smiled at Arryn. "That's so awesome! I don't think I could be a warrior, though. I don't understand how you can take that much pain. That sounds horrible."

Arryn smiled. "Well, if you want, you can stick around. If you don't want to see, you don't have to. The Chieftain will have more than enough for you to do."

"Here, when a boy or girl is old enough to hold a spear, they are old enough to start training. You're old enough for basics, but the rougher training won't start until after twelve," Nika said.

"Rougher training?" Corrine asked.

Cathillian nodded. "There's still a lot for you to learn. Don't worry about all that right now. If you want, you can watch Arryn and me spar today. Arryn and Nika are supposed to be demonstrating, but I think it would be good for you to see a woman fight a man much larger than her."

Arryn looked impressed. "Wow. Actually, that's a really good idea. See, I'm a shorty compared to everyone here. They are all tall and long-limbed, but I'm not a native druid. I'm built like the shorter Arcadians. You're more than welcome to stay if you want, but you don't have to."

Corrine thought for a few moments. "I wanna watch. I don't

think I'll like it, but if I'm gonna be a druid of the Dark Forest, I should at least see what goes on."

"Just don't be scared when he hits me or draws blood… or worse. Trust me, I'll get him back," Arryn said with a wink.

"Yeah," Cathillian agreed. "You always do. You're mean, too."

Arryn gave him a playful punch in the shoulder before stepping into the pit.

Cathillian looked at Corrine. "Wish me luck. I'm gonna need it. She's gonna show off in front of you. Just you wait."

Corrine smiled. "You're a big boy. I'm sure you can handle it."

His expression turned shocked. "Well, look at you! You're already just as mean as she is. What a pair you two are!"

He winked as he turned and followed Arryn into the pit.

"Today, I think we should try something a little different," Nika said. When Arryn, Cathillian, and Corrine all looked at her, she smiled. "The two of you are great fighters already. Let's see just how far we can push you. Let's see how you do *blindfolded*."

Arryn stared at Nika in shock. "Blindfolded? That doesn't sound safe."

Nika shook her head. "No weapons. Hand-to-hand only. It should test your ability to sense life around you. If you're as good with your nature magic as Cathillian is, you won't have anything to worry about. You'll be able to sense where he is at all times."

Cathillian clapped his hands, grinning deviously as he rubbed them together. "What's the matter? Are you scared? Afraid you might *lose*?"

Arryn snorted. "Really? Never! Bring on the blindfolds. But *Nika* will tie them."

Cathillian nodded. "That seems fair."

Nika removed two blindfolds from her belt, having placed them there in preparation for this very event. Arryn narrowed her eyes as she realized the warrior had planned this from the beginning.

"Do you normally carry scarves with you, or did you plan to

blindfold me today anyway? Because as Cathillian mentioned earlier, it was supposed to be you and me in the pit today."

Nika laughed as she stepped behind Arryn, tying the blindfold. "I definitely had this planned. We've become such evenly matched opponents, I wanted to see what you're capable of if we shook things up. If anything, it's a compliment."

"Mmhmm," Arryn grumbled as she took a few steps backwards, carefully placing her feet and sensing around her, so she didn't run into anything.

"Okay, Cathillian's blindfolded as well. I'm gonna count to three, and then the fight is on. If someone goes down for more than a few seconds, I'll call it. Any questions?"

Arryn shook her head, assuming that Cathillian had as well because Nika began the countdown.

"*Go!*" Nika shouted.

Arryn called on her magic, both physical and nature. Her physical magic allowed her to sense vibrations in the ground while her nature magic allowed her to sense Cathillian's life energy. Once he called on his magic, she could sense that as well.

She slowly began to circle him, feeling for Corrine and Nika just outside the pit. That told her where the pit ended on that side.

Cathillian—impatient as he was—was the first to attack. She sensed him coming, but it was too late to move, so she caught a fist directly to her nose. The sound of bone breaking echoed in her ears as the pain radiated through her head.

"Ah, Bitch!" she shouted as she punched him in the ribs and then kicked out, hitting him directly in the chest only by luck.

"Arryn! Are you okay?" Corrine asked, worry evident in her voice.

Arryn gripped her nose hard enough to straighten it, and the sound of grinding bone once again hit her ears as the pain gave her an instant headache. She then pinched just the soft cartilage and pulled downward, flinging the blood away from her face and off her fingertips at the ground.

"Don't worry about me, kid," Arryn said. "It's just a broken nose. Trust me, that's not a mistake I'm gonna make again."

"What? No worries for my broken ribs?" Cathillian grumbled.

"Are you okay, Cathillian?" Corrine asked.

"Na, na, na. It's too late for that. I see where your allegiance lies," he replied.

Arryn focused her magic again, using his distraction to her benefit. No one had been taken down, and Nika hadn't signaled the end of the round. If he was distracted, it was his own fault.

She found where he was standing, and he didn't seem to be moving. She quickly judged how far he was and figured how many steps it would take to get to him, and then she made a risky move.

Arryn dropped her nature magic, making it a little harder for him to sense her, and she ran directly for him. Just as she arrived, she called her magic again, which told her that he was still there.

Thrusting a knee into his side as he leaned toward her, she wrapped her arm around his neck and threw him over her back to the ground, where she straddled him after he landed. She could feel him struggling upward, but she stopped him with a swift punch to the face.

"Fuck!" Cathillian yelled as his nose was crushed by her fist.

Arryn heard laughing just before Nika said, "The element of surprise really brings out the cursing. This is the best idea ever. Also, round over. Point to Arryn. Nice, by the way—dropping your nature magic. It was a risk, but it paid off."

Arryn patted Cathillian on the chest, and his hand went to cover it. When she felt his touch, she grabbed his hand, stood, and helped pull him to his feet.

"So, Arryn won?" Corrine asked.

Arryn nodded. "That round, anyway. Are we continuing with the blindfolds, or can we just train?"

"Yeah, I'd rather just train the good old-fashioned way. Seems like she hits twice as hard with a blindfold on," Cathillian said.

Nika groaned. "Fine, ya whiners. Take the blindfolds off. Since you can see now, no rules. Hand-to-hand, weapons, magic —whatever you wanna use."

Arryn removed her blindfold and glanced at Corrine, who had her hands on the railing that encircled the pit. Her eyes were aglow with excitement, and she had a big smile on her face.

Arryn winked at the girl before turning back to her opponent. "Round two, ya big baby. Let's see what ya got."

Cathillian put his fists up in a fighter's stance as he prepared for Arryn. This time she took the initiative.

Her eyes flashed black before Cathillian had time to react. She swept her hand forward and to the left, flinging large clods of dirt directly at him. He closed his eyes and used his arms to cover his face, and she charged straight for him, then jumped into the air and mule-kicked him in the chest. She used that momentum to somersault off him and landed on her feet.

Cathillian stumbled back several steps, but caught his balance and flipped backwards, landing on his feet. He steadied himself, and his eyes flashed as he thrust his hands out, sending a large gust of wind to knock Arryn back.

She hit the ground hard, but quickly rolled onto all fours to keep Nika from calling the round and flung her hand backward. Vines burst from the ground and grabbed Cathillian by the ankles.

When she yanked her hand back toward her, the vines pulled his feet out from under him and he landed with a loud *oof*. Arryn climbed to her feet and ran for him, but before she had even made it halfway, he had sliced the vines and freed himself.

He rolled out of the way, sweep-kicking her legs. She landed flat on her stomach with a loud grunt as he straddled her back, grabbed her hands, and pinned her.

"Sorry, Arryn," Nika called. "Point to Cathillian."

"*Boo!*" Corrine shouted.

"Hey!" Cathillian exclaimed as he looked at her, rolling off Arryn so she could sit up. The girl laughed as she continued to jeer, and he declared, "You just wait, little one. I'll remember this."

Arryn laughed and slugged him in the arm. "See? Everyone likes me better. Maybe it's because I'm nicer."

Cathillian chuckled. "You're full of shit, is what you are."

They heard voices in the distance as the experienced warriors led the students toward the pit for the day's training. Many brought weapons, placing them in the various racks at the edges of the arena as they greeted Nika warmly. Some stopped to talk to Corrine as well.

"I suppose that means your time is up," Nika said, motioning for them to leave the pit.

Arryn looked at Cathillian. "We'll finish this later."

He gave her a wink and a mischievous smile. "Is that a promise?"

She shook her head as she made her way out of the pit. "You really are ridiculous," she called back.

When she reached Corrine, the young girl was talking with a few of the warrior recruits. They were some of the newest students in the most basic training, since they were the same age as her.

Corrine was telling them she couldn't believe a woman could fight so well, let alone against a man that size. A few of the other children laughed, and one of them put her arm around her.

"You're still new around here, so there's a lot you don't know. You should join our class. Since you already have a talent for using vines, maybe you'd be interested in the *Schatten*," the girl, whose name was Molly, said.

"What're the *Schatten*?" Corrine asked.

Arryn smiled. "They're actually the coolest warriors in the village. They use subtlety. Essentially, they're trained assassins. They don't get to see as much action as the rest of us, but when they do they're amazing as hell. Molly is saying that because you already use one of the forms of magic they do, and you're extremely quiet while doing it, you might be very suited to their skills."

Her eyes widened, and a smile spread. "You really think so? I didn't think training sounded like a very good idea earlier, but after watching you and Cathillian fight and hearing about the *Schatten*, I think I wanna be a warrior."

Arryn smiled. "Then you'll fit in just fine. You might even be able to teach these guys a few things."

Arryn and Corrine both turned when they heard Nika calling out names to make sure all the students were in attendance.

"We'll talk about this later. Hang out with us for the day, so you can see how the kids your age train. By the time you're old enough for the training that involves physical pain, you'll already have enough bumps and bruises under your belt from falls and mishaps with bamboo training staffs that a broken nose won't seem like much of anything."

The young girl nodded. "I can't wait."

CHAPTER SEVEN

melia checked in at the factory, making sure everything was up and running and in order. The city had been slowly getting back into a routine. It was still far from normal, but mostly people were just happy to be working again. It allowed them to get their minds off everything that had happened.

And even with the bandits wreaking havoc down south on the rearick trade caravans, shipments of brew and amphoralds had been coming in steadily. Taking care of the problem with the violent thieves on the main road was her next course of action.

Except for this one.

It was a big day. Well, a big day for Elon, anyway. It had taken him a couple days to decide, but he had finally made up his mind. He wanted to find Gregory and apologize to him face to face, no matter what the consequences.

Amelia was proud of him for making the decision, knowing it wouldn't be easy. It had been nearly a year since Elon had seen Gregory, and there was no way for him to know just how much hate the young man still held in his heart for his father, or how much he had changed himself.

When he thought back on it, Elon had spent years making Gregory feel worthless. In the end, Gregory was a better man than he had ever thought about being.

It was a shame Elon hadn't acknowledged his son's worth earlier, because Gregory had his father's talent for all things technical. He had a passion in him much like Elon's own when it came to learning how things worked and inventing new things.

Amelia knew Elon hoped Gregory would forgive him, so that he could mentor his son as Waylon had mentored him. It was a hobby they could both share, one that might allow them to start a brand-new life somewhere else.

As Amelia made her way to the city gate, she looked at the trees the druids had grown on the day of battle. Instead of cutting them down for lumber as had originally been planned, the city council had very recently decided to keep them. They rebuilt the road around them, leaving a gap in the stones around the trees for the trunks to grow.

Now, instead of rubble and the remains of battle inside the city walls, there was a majestic row of trees with thick, vividly green leaves that added to the city's beauty. They had been able to rebuild the street wide enough on each side to allow carriages to pass.

Amelia loved the newest addition, even if it had come from something terrible.

As usual, there were four guards at the gate, each of them casually talking with Elon. It had been a long time since she had seen him genuinely smile. He seemed to be truly happy, and that made her feel optimistic for him.

His eyes wandered over to her, and his smile grew as he waved. Waylon was leaning against the wall near him for support.

"Good morning, Governor," Elon said. "I'm surprised you could make it."

She waved a hand in the air. "Wouldn't miss it for the world. I just had to make an appearance at the factory. I wanted to make sure everything is going well."

Elon nodded. "I'll take your sunny disposition as a sign that it is. Glad to hear it."

She laughed. "It is, yes. It's taking time, but I think people are starting to come back around. I doubt very seriously the scars of what happened will heal anytime soon, and maybe they never will. But getting on with their lives is a great start."

He briefly looked at his feet before returning his gaze to her. "I want to thank you. You have no idea exactly what you've done for me. It means a lot for me to have the opportunity to find my son. He's with Hannah, so I know he's safe. I have no doubt about that. Most of all, it means the world to have someone believe in me again, and for the right reasons this time."

Waylon stepped away from the wall and rested his hand on Elon's back. "You always had the support of good people, son. You just had shitty taste in friends, and looked up to the wrong people."

The corner of Elon's mouth turned up as he looked at his mentor. "Are you saying *you're* the wrong people?"

Waylon looked at him incredulously. "What? No! Of course, not. I'm *amazing*. In fact, I'm *exactly* who you should've been looking up to this whole time, not that asshat Adrien."

Elon and Amelia both laughed. "He's right. You did have terrible taste in friends, but it seems like you've learned your lesson," she said.

He nodded. "I should certainly think so. If someone does something nice for someone else only when other people are watching, or only when it will be told to other people—probably not the best person to have around. Also, if they seem hungry for more power, that's probably not a good sign either." His voice was light and amused.

It was different, seeing him with the ability to joke about everything that had happened and his bad choices. She had a feeling it was mostly for their benefit, but after all, he couldn't change what happened. Working to better himself and finding new ways to laugh would be pretty good therapy. He really did seem like a brand-new person.

"You will always have a home here, you know," Amelia said.

He nodded and pulled her into a hug. Her eyes widened for a moment when he wrapped his arms around her, but she quickly relaxed into the embrace.

He drew back and held his hand up before stepping over to Waylon. After a few moments, he returned with a familiar-looking box, which he handed to Amelia. It was just like the ones from before, and bore Waylon's design and mark.

Suspecting what might be inside, she was very careful while opening it. As expected, her eyes were met by the familiar glow of magitech.

"It's all new. We did it! We figured out how to extend the blast radius while keeping the core cooled. It'll need a recharge period just like before, but it will still blast ten times before it needs to cool. I dropped the blueprints at the factory before I came down here, but I told him to wait until tomorrow to ask you for production instructions."

She smiled as she looked from the deadly magitech mine in the box to Elon. "Thank you. These will help everyone feel more secure. I figure we'll bury a couple hundred on our borders and mark them with trees. We can tell our people what they are, but they'll keep the remnant out. I also plan to assign guards to patrol that area, out of the blast zone, but close enough to keep any wanderers from getting hurt."

Elon nodded and smiled. "I'm glad I could help. Take care of yourself, Amelia. Take care of the city. They need you now more than ever."

"You, too, Elon," Amelia replied.

They finished saying their goodbyes, and Amelia and Waylon

watched as Elon climbed on the back of a beautiful mare that Amelia had gifted to him the day before and rode off.

Waylon came to stand at Amelia's side, sighing before turning and pointing at the box with a devious smile. "Wanna go bury it and drop a heavy rock on it?"

Amelia was shocked when she saw how excited and alive he looked at the thought of causing some trouble. When her shock wore off, she shook her head. For a moment, the old man looked disappointed.

But then Amelia gave a devious smile of her own and said, "I get to drop the rock."

LEAVING KEMET, their home, had been a big decision for Bast and Cleo, but they hadn't had much choice because the Arcadian Valley was not the only place in Irth to encounter trouble. Strange things had been happening, and the lives of their people were in danger. Because of that, their mother, Nailah, had sent them away in hope they would both be safe as well as find help.

Life in the desert had always been hard, but their people were strong. They could take care of themselves for the most part, and they had lived peacefully in their small city since before the Age of Madness.

They had built strong homes using heavy stones, the largest of those homes being pyramids. Their walls had been built strongly enough that not even the remnant could get inside. They could house and protect many families if need be.

But it appeared there were more things to fear out there than remnant or the occasional lycanthrope.

The twin girls were the fastest runners in their community, and their horses were, too. That was why they had been chosen above all others to travel northwest to the Mystic Temple to find help.

A few years before, traveling mystics had come through Kemet and told them stories of their Temple as well as the city that had been built with magic.

According to the mystics, the Temple was full of men and women just like them, mental magicians who specialized in illusions, storytelling, and making one hell of a good brew.

With everything going on in Kemet, the girls needed help, but not just anyone would do. They needed skilled and masterful magicians, those with the strength and expertise to deal with such situations. Even her people's strength hadn't been enough to help them, and they didn't have warriors in their city.

Bast and Cleo traveled as quickly as they could, but it still took two weeks to travel across the western desert to the sea and find a ship willing to take them and their horses across it to the land in which the Arcadian Valley and the Heights were located.

When they finally arrived at the Temple, they had been greeted by a mystic named Margit, who offered them food and a warm bed. Their stay was much shorter than they had imagined it would be, but it had still been helpful.

The mystics were awaiting the return of their master, and could offer no assistance other than to point them toward Arcadia. That city had seen many troubles of its own, but was finally under the control of a woman who had the people's best interests at heart.

"Travel to Arcadia and speak to a woman named Amelia. She has a strong mind, and a strong heart. I can't promise she'll be able to help you directly because she's recently fought a battle of her own, but if nothing else she'll be able to point you in the right direction," Margit had told them.

Bast and Cleo had spent the night talking with Margit and the others about the mystics who had visited their land and all they had learned from them. While they talked, ate, and rested, their horses had been cared for as well, fed and sheltered against the night.

Early the following morning, they were given a large break-fast and a friendly send-off. The mystics were kind and generous people, and the twins wanted to stop back by on their way home —hopefully with a group of experienced fighters.

After saying their goodbyes, Bast and Cleo retrieved their horses and set off once again—this time to Arcadia, which they hoped would be their final destination.

After passing through a small rearick town called Craigston, they made their way down the mountain, where they rode toward the great city of magicians. It would take a bit longer to hit flat land, but they had nearly reached the hills at the bottom.

"We've traveled all this way," Bast said to her twin sister. Using her legs, she squeezed her horse's sides, urging the mare to move a bit faster to keep pace with Cleo's mount. "Part of me feels this long-ass trip will leave us empty-handed. The other part of me thinks we'll find exactly what we need in Arcadia. I'm worried, Sister."

Cleo nodded. "We have no way of knowing what's happening back in Kemet right now. For some reason, that's scarier for you than it is for me. I guess deep down, I feel like Mama can handle it until we get back, but we've gotta have faith. She wouldn't have sent us for help if she hadn't truly believed we would find it."

Bast nodded. "Let's hope you're right. She could have just sent us away, so we didn't have to watch the city fall. Whether we find help or not, I'm scared to return home."

Even though Bast hadn't said what she meant, Cleo knew exactly what she was worried about. She was terrified that when they went home they would find everyone they had ever loved dead. "I know. Me, too."

They rode in silence for quite a while, each of them wondering what they might find in the grand city. Bast found herself contemplating the culinary treats the city might have to offer, but she promptly felt bad for thinking of fancy food during such an important mission.

Still… A girl had to eat, right?

Cleo pulled back on the reins of her horse, the animal grunting in protest as it slowed to a stop. Bast was quick to stop her horse as well.

"What is it?" Bast asked.

Cleo's face was fraught with worry. "Do you hear that? Sounds like clashing metal."

Bast turned, her eyes narrowing a bit as she listened intently. As they were leaving Craigston, they had seen a group of rearick packing up to travel to Arcadia, but they couldn't possibly have been the source of the sound.

She had overheard them say they didn't plan to leave for a few hours. That would have put them miles behind her and Cleo.

Then she heard yelling and the sounds of battle. Her eyes locked onto her sister's for a moment, and they urged their horses into a full gallop.

"I heard they had been having problems with bandits on the road for a few weeks now," Cleo shouted over the hoofbeats, "but I never thought we would run directly into them."

"Me neither!" Bast replied. "I think it's time we made ourselves useful."

Cleo smiled dangerously. "I couldn't agree more."

As they reached the bottom of the mountain, they saw a group of ten or so rearick taking on nearly twice their number of bandits. The smaller rearick men were armed with hammers and blunt weapons, but the larger men were armed with sharp knives and swords.

While Bast didn't have extensive knowledge or experience with rearick, the mystics had spoken highly of them, and the ones they had met going through Craigston had been rough and sarcastic, but friendly.

Her kind of people.

She would be damned before she let hardworking, honest

people be taken down by bastards like those, men who stole from folk who earned their way in life.

Bast couldn't wait to show them exactly why they shouldn't pick on the little guy.

The girls brought their horses to a hard stop, dismounting and positioning themselves about ten feet from the main battle. By the time they reached the fight, the men had the rearick on their knees, blades to their throats.

The girls looked at one another and Cleo turned back to the fight. "Hey, fellas!"

A tall man on the edge of the battle had been about to bring a sword down on one of the rearick, but he stopped and turned to face them, immediately beginning to laugh.

"Get outta here, lasses!" one of the rearick said. "Save yerselves!"

Bast took a step forward when she saw one of the men punch the rearick who had warned her. "Oh, sweetheart. You shouldn't've done that," she said coldly to the offender.

The man smiled, showing that one of his front teeth was missing—more than likely from that very battle, judging by the blood on his remaining teeth.

"Is that so?" He took a step toward her and smiled even bigger as he took another, exaggerating each movement. "Well, gorgeous, I'm right here. I'll even give you the first shot before I teach you a lesson in respect."

He laughed again as he tapped his jaw, turning his face just slightly as an invite. "Come on, little lady. First shot."

The other men surrounding the rearick laughed heartily, egging her on and making condescending remarks at her expense.

She saw the desperation on the rearick's faces as they stared at the girls. She had heard they were a protective lot, and she could see it in the way they silently pleaded with her to run.

She took a few steps forward, leaving only an arm's reach

between them. The man in front of her towered over her five-foot frame, but that didn't matter to her.

Her fists clenched at her side and her mind wandered to the lives at stake back in her land. Innocent people going about their business and trying to do right, in danger from beasts that had no compassion.

This man may have been human, but he was no different.

And there was nothing Bast or her sister hated worse than assholes who had no respect for life.

She felt a familiar tingle travel through her arm and down into her hand, signaling she was ready. She gave a broad smile as she lightly shook her head, her eyes flashing bright blue as she did. "You're *really* gonna wish you hadn't told me to do this."

Bast's fist hit him directly in the jaw, power exploding from her hand. She felt the bone in his face disintegrate under the blow and he was thrown several feet back. He screamed in pain as he hit the ground, but was unable to continue when the air was knocked out of him.

Her smile grew darker as she turned to the large group of men, arms rising out from her sides briefly as she said, "So, who's next?"

Another man ran directly for her, this one much broader and even a little taller than the other. He looked like he had been on a farm most of his life.

Her eyes grew bluer as she dropped to the ground, punching him directly in the knee with the same strength as before. The joint and epiphyses of the surrounding bones shattered, and she stood and drove her fist hard into his face, power once again exploding out of her hand. Just as his friend had before him, he flew several feet back and hit the ground.

His face was crushed in behind his broken nose, and his eyes were open and stared blankly. There was no doubt in her mind he was dead, but that didn't matter. She saw at least two dead rearick on the ground, so he had deserved it.

"Hey, fellas, don't let me keep you all to myself! I bet my sister would just *love* to get to know you better. Right, Sis?" Bast asked, glancing at the other girl.

As Cleo stepped forward, the rims of her irises started to turn blue and the darkness of the color began to slowly bleed into the natural green of her eyes. She gave the same dark smile her sister had as she stepped forward, balling her right hand into a fist and lightly punching it into her left palm.

"Oh, yes. There's plenty of us to go around, boys," she said with a wink.

The men looked at one another with fear in their expressions, their gazes darting to the much smaller but still terrifying teenage girls as they debated hard about what they should do.

Cleo turned to Bast, poking her bottom lip out as if she were pouting. "Aw, Bast, I don't think they like me."

Bast's jaw dropped open in feigned horror. "That's just rude. Maybe we should just make the first move."

Cleo laughed. "Yeah. Karma's a bitch, boys. I think it's time you met her."

The bandits turned and ran, but that only made things easier for the girls. They now had clear shots, because the men were no longer holding blades to the rearick's throats.

They were free to attack.

Both Cleo and Bast charged after them, channeling their power through their feet as they sprinted. Their magic propelled them forward, making their strides several times longer than their much taller opponents and allowed them to move faster than any other human they had ever met.

Cleo jumped, landing on the back of one of the men and taking him to the ground, where they rolled several times before coming to a stop. She leapt up to her feet, diving forward and punching him hard in the stomach with her normal strength, though it was enough to do the job.

He stumbled back several feet before falling, curling up in a ball as he struggled to breathe.

She turned and ran for another, but was confronted with a sword. She jumped out of the way just in time to avoid the brunt of the hit, but it still slashed across her chest. She cried out in pain, but her anger at being injured only drove her harder.

Charging forward, she ducked another swing, coming up to hit her attacker hard in the ribs as she channeled a blast of power through her fist and directly into him.

He dropped the sword and clutched his side as he gasped for air. She had no doubt she had punctured his lung with one of his broken ribs, but she also knew he wasn't going to have to worry about it much longer. She snatched the sword and swung, slicing clean through his neck.

At that point, the rearick were back in the fight again, swinging hammers and kicking asses again.

Bast shoved one of her opponents away to allow her to deal with the other, kneeing him in the groin before delivering a power-packed punch to the side of his head, which dropped him.

As the first one recovered from the shove, he charged at her, but she was prepared. She caught him completely off-guard when she did a front handspring, wrapping her legs around his head before folding up and punching him hard in the face.

As he fell backward, she slid down his body and rolled to her feet. The last two men were being taken down by the rearick. As soon as they were out of commission, she and her sister went over to the rearick.

"The rest of you guys okay? I know you lost a couple, but how are the rest of you?" Bast asked.

Cleo clutched her chest, the blood from the wound not really showing up against her black shirt.

One of the rearick pointed. "We got some bumps and bruises, but yer sis there is the one ta worry 'bout."

Bast's eyes went wide when the gap in her sister's shirt

revealed a long gash. "Cleo, are you okay?" she asked as she rushed to her side.

An older rearick broke through the others and walked over, both old and new battle scars covering his face and down his arms.

"I don't mean ta look at yer goods, young lass, but I've seen me fair share o' battles an' battle wounds. Let me take a gander. I ain't no healer, but I can sure patch ye up good enough ta get ya back ta a med bed in Craigston. Maybe even ta Arcadia if it ain't too bad."

Cleo dropped to her knees, exhausted from the magic use and weak from blood loss. She turned her back to the others while the older rearick pulled her shirt back to examine her. He was careful to keep her breasts covered as he looked at the places that were bleeding the worst.

"It needs stitches, lass, but ye'll be fine. I've done 'em enough times. I can do it for ye, or I can tell yer sis how ta do it. I understand if ye're more comfortable with her."

Bast knelt next to the rearick and across from her sister. "I've put stitches in my own wounds by myself, but I've never put any in someone else. Let him do it. I don't want to make things worse."

Cleo nodded, not really having the energy to argue with anyone at the moment. "Thank you…"

"The name's Sven," the rearick replied.

"Well, thank you, Sven. I appreciate you helping me," Cleo said weakly.

The rearick was standing now, and he smiled and shook his head. "Lass, if not fer ye and yer sis here, we'd all be dead. A stitch or two is the least I can do."

Sven went back to his group and gave them orders to separate their own dead from the rest and get them in the carts. He grabbed an emergency pack and carried it back before kneeling in front of Cleo again. He handed her a large jug before opening the pack.

"What's that?" Cleo asked as she took it. She had to use both hands to hold it.

He smiled as he dug through his bag. "That's whiskey," he replied with a bit of amusement in his voice. "Ye'll wanna take a few drinks o' that. Big 'uns. This ain't gonna be pleasant, 'specially when I dump some o' that across yer chest ta clean the wound. It appears I left me antiseptic back in town."

The sisters looked at one another, wide-eyed, and Bast shrugged. "The mystics *did* tell us the rearick made good booze."

Sven laughed. "It might taste like a bucket o' goat's piss that's had rusty nails soakin' in it fer a week in the hot sun, but it's sure as hell effective."

Cleo glanced at him in disgust.

Bast smiled. "*And* they said they were interesting people."

Cleo shook her head as she lifted the jug to her mouth, pausing before taking a sip. "Is this shit strong enough to kill the pain?"

He shook his head and smiled as he threaded the needle. "Lass, that's strong enough ta make ye forget it tastes like shite. Now, start drinkin', 'cuz I'm 'bout ta start stitchin' ye from shoulder ta rib."

Cleo hissed in pain as she sat up a little straighter. "Sounds like this is gonna be a fun day." She tilted the jug back with both hands, taking several big gulps while trying not to throw up.

CHAPTER EIGHT

During Arryn's downtimes, she had been working with Corrine on her healing skills. It took patience, but between her lessons with Arryn and being in the Chieftain's healing class with the other children, she was picking it up fast.

Today, however, Arryn decided she wanted to take a little time for herself. Every day, she dedicated all her time to everyone else from the moment she woke to the time she went to sleep.

Although she trained in combat techniques with Nika, Elysia, and Cathillian, today she wanted to work on her magic, some of which couldn't be taught by the others. She had to teach herself.

Midday, while Arryn was supposed to be relaxing and enjoying her hour to herself, she went to the river. She loved the water, and the river had always been a beautiful spot—but today wouldn't be for rest.

Arryn wore nothing but a pair of leather shorts and a tight-fitting shirt, clothing that was suitable for swimming if her practice went badly. She stepped to the water, her toes sinking into the little bit of sand along its edge.

She took a deep breath and held it for a moment before slowly blowing it out, her eyes closing as she focused. When she opened them, they had turned black, and her power encircled her.

Carefully, she touched her toe to the surface of the water, freezing it solid as she slowly put weight on it. As her foot pressed down, the ice dipped under the surface, and the current immediately carried it away.

She sighed as she realized she was going to have to put a bit more effort into it. Taking another deep breath, she once again touched her toes to the surface, the water again freezing under her foot.

She pushed harder, the ice growing downward until it meshed with the bed of the river.

Arryn cautiously placed her weight on the ice again, but this time its wide base was buried deep in the dirt and rock beneath the water and it held her steady. She moved her other foot forward, daring to take another step onto the surface and repeating the process.

By the time she reached the center of the river, she was heavily regretting not having worn shoes. She looked at the edge, just where the grass began, and saw her warrior clothing lying there.

Stretching out her hand, she levitated her pants over to her, and quickly folded them and placed them on the ice beneath her feet.

She didn't feel quite as connected to the water as she had before, but she took that as a challenge. Focusing hard on the ice below her, she imagined it as a steady pillar below her feet, digging deeply into the river bed.

The trouble was that the water was warm and rushing quickly. If she didn't focus, the river would dissolve her steady pillar in a matter of seconds.

Once she had held it for a minute or two, she decided to challenge herself.

"What are you doing?" Celine asked.

Arryn almost slipped from the distraction. She had been focusing so hard on what she was doing that she had completely forgotten to pay attention to her surroundings.

"Nearly shitting my pants, that's what. You scared the hell out of me."

Celine laughed. "Sorry about that. I heard you headed off in this direction, and I wanted to check on you and make sure you were okay. You don't usually blow everyone off."

Arryn took a couple of deep breaths, centering herself again as she added more ice to the platform. It had already begun to melt with her distraction.

"That's very true, but today I just felt like I needed to train myself. I don't have a physical magic teacher, so the only way I'm going to learn is by practicing. When I came to the Dark Forest, I tried to learn by myself, but it never worked. I could do a couple of things, but that was it. I feel much more open to magic now."

"Well, you have certainly learned a *lot* since then, especially in the last few months. So, I guess we are focusing on water today?" Celine asked. "You want me to leave you alone?"

Arryn shook her head. "No, actually I can use the distraction. It's good for training, so you're more than welcome to hang out and talk to me if you want. And yes, I'm working with ice. I remember seeing Mom practice when I was little. She was always best with fire and ice."

"Yeah, you have no idea. When we were younger, I used to pick on her *all* the time. I was the typical bratty sister. I'd steal her hair clips and hide them in the horse stalls. When she found them, they'd be covered in horse shit."

Arryn started laughing. "You seriously did that to her? That's terrible! Actually, that sounds like something I would do to Cathillian."

"Hey, she deserved it! She ruined my favorite dress. She flicked ink all over it from my father's inkwell, and I had nothing to wear to the big dinner that night. One night she got so mad at me that she set my bed on fire."

Arryn's eyes widened as she looked at her aunt. She felt a wobble in her ice platform and realized she had lost concentration completely on hearing that her mother had nearly killed Celine in a fit of rage.

"Whoa," Arryn said, focusing again. "She must've been pretty pissed off."

She took a deep breath and slowly blew it out, lifting her hands from her sides and keeping her palms flat and facing the water.

"Well, I *might* have destroyed a few things of Dad's and then told him it was her. She got in *so* much trouble for that. She had been out with your father that night. It was the first night they'd really spent any time together, and Dad said she was not allowed to see him again for a month. Boy oh boy, was she ever pissed at me."

Arryn smiled as she listened to the story. It made her happy to hear about any of her family, but especially about her mother and father when they were young.

Keeping her focus on the rushing water as well as the ice below her, Arryn lifted her hands slowly, bringing ribbons of water up to her palms. She threw out her right hand, attempting to sling the water like a whip, but instead she completely lost her balance.

The ice below her disappeared as she landed flat on her back in the waist-deep water and was immediately swallowed by it. As she fought the heavy current to come up to the surface, the water surrounding her swirled and froze, lifting her to safety and carrying her to edge of the river.

As the ice set her down on the shore, she saw Celine's eyes fade back to their normal color. Her aunt flipped her hand toward the river, sending the water cascading back into it.

"Your mom wasn't the only one who was really good with

water and ice," Celine said with a wink. "Don't be afraid to ask me questions. I'm not as good as she was, but I still might be able to help."

Arryn was still breathing heavily from the combination of magic fatigue and being under the water. She laughed, realizing just how stubborn she had been. She felt as though she had relied on everyone else so much while growing up, and even as an adult, that when she finally figured out how to do things for herself, that was the way it should be.

But it didn't have to be.

Asking for help didn't make her weak, and it didn't make her needy. It made her smart and resourceful. Her community thrived entirely on the push and pull of asking for and giving help. There was no reason she should be any different.

In fact, she felt a little embarrassed.

Arryn nodded. "Thank you. Sometimes I feel like I should try things on my own before I ask for help."

Celine laughed. "That's exactly how *bad* things happen. Had I not been here, you could've busted your head on a rock when you fell and drowned."

Arryn briefly looked at the river before meeting her aunt's gaze. At that moment, Celine looked just like Arryn's mother. "Trust me, I won't be doing that again. Well, not alone, anyway."

"I'm glad to hear it. So, how are things?" Celine's eyes flashed black as her hands briefly lifted in front of her, the tips of her fingers touching before she pulled her hands apart. The water that had soaked Arryn lifted free of her body and hair, leaving her dry. Celine dropped her hands and the water fell to the ground as her eyes returned to normal.

"Things are good," Arryn said. "But I know what you're trying to do, and it's not going to work. How about we change tactics? How are you and *Samuel*? Speaking of good ol' Sam, where is *he* this lovely afternoon?"

Both Celine and Arryn turned east to make their way back to

the village. Arryn stopped to pick up her training shirt and boots before going any farther.

"If you tell him I told you, he'll kill me, so keep your mouth shut. But he's with the Chieftain. It's downtime for everyone, so he and the Chieftain are training."

Arryn looked at her curiously. "Training? Hand-to-hand or healing?"

Celine looked at her with a shocked expression. "How did you know?"

Arryn winked. "I'm a good judge of ability, and sometimes I just sense things. I can tell when someone is a good person, which was what led me to hate Talia so much, and I can also sense magic. That's kind of a druid thing, though. In fact, I'm sure if you asked any druid here who knows Sam, they'd tell you they could sense the ability in him."

Celine laughed. "You guys are all just being nice to him and not saying anything, aren't you?"

Arryn shrugged. "Honestly, it's my nature to give him a hard time, but I don't for the same reason everyone else here doesn't. Even Cathillian hasn't mentioned it, as far as I know. The rearick hate magic with a passion. They just don't understand it. If we picked on him about his curiosity and desire to learn, he would stop immediately. And his motives are pure, so we don't want that."

"That's really nice of you guys, especially Cathillian. I'm really quite shocked he hasn't said anything, because he and Samuel are always giving each other a hard time."

Arryn laughed. "Oh, trust me, the time is getting near. Once Cathillian figures that Sam knows what he's doing and that it won't matter if he quits or not, he'll start picking on him pretty good."

Celine just grimaced.

Groaning, Arryn said, "I need to stop by my house before going back to the pit, or I'm going to be fighting in leather short shorts. I guess it *would* be pretty funny, but I'm trying to make a good impression on the younger guys. They need their asses kicked twice as hard because they think they're studs and better than everyone else."

"Well, it would also turn Cathillian's head," Celine said, waggling her brows.

Arryn stopped, smiling briefly before shaking her head. "One of these days, but not today."

CHAPTER NINE

Once the sun had set on the Dark Forest, and everyone was exhausted from their day, the younger children were put to bed while the older children were given the opportunity to join the adults around fire to listen to the next section of the Chieftain's story.

The Chieftain once again held his two mugs of wine and smiled as everyone gathered around. Zoe had spent the day with him, watching as he taught the young ones how to work with vines. It was one of their most precious fighting tools, and it would come in handy for many reasons—especially at their age.

Little Corrine had been quite a help in that department. She had taught them some of her techniques, and explained how the vines could be used by kids who were still too little to fight. Getting away quickly and hiding in the trees was a much better option for them.

Once they had practiced for a while, Zoe had asked the Chieftain if she might train them a bit on mental barriers. Given everything that had happened in Arcadia, Zoe felt it was a worthwhile thing for them to learn.

She would still be there for a few more days, and she wanted to help in more ways than just lending her talents to storytelling.

The Chieftain allowed her to teach the students how to meditate, as well as create a strong mental barrier. Both those things would take quite a lot of practice, but Zoe was confident she could teach them the basics over the course of a couple days.

The mystic came to stand by the Chieftain's side as she had every night, ready to play her part. Once everyone was seated, the Chieftain took one last long drink from his wine and addressed everyone.

"Thank you, everyone, for joining us again. When we left off, Alaric had disobeyed my orders and gone off on his own, resulting in the deaths of two of our people. Also, my wife and I had just discovered we were to be parents again."

The Chieftain looked at his daughter, Elysia, and smiled. She smiled back.

"I'm going to skip a couple of years, not because they aren't important, but because if I told you every small thing Alaric did to reinforce my convictions of trouble, we would be here for weeks, and we simply don't have that kind of time. In short, I should have removed him a long time before I did.

"Over those two years, I caught him in many lies. In training courses, he would belittle the children and threaten them. He believed patience was for the weak. I didn't know about it for a very long time, until a fellow warrior caught him threatening to make training even harder if the kids told me. I spied on him, unable to believe it could be true, but I saw it with my own eyes."

The Chieftain smiled and waved away the plate of fruit Arryn offered him before she sat down in her regular place next to Celine, Elysia, Cathillian, and Samuel. She shared the fruit among her friends and family.

The Chieftain cleared his throat and continued, "The final straw came just over three years after we started our lives here. Trading with Arcadia had become very difficult, to say the least.

Adrien demanded more and more, and I knew it was only a matter of time before he threatened us.

"In that short amount of time, we had already developed a reputation. We trained day in and day out, just as we do now. Our physical appearance had changed. Our eyes had turned from their natural color to various shades of green. Our ears had become slightly longer and pointed at the top, and our skin and hair had become healthier.

"The physical changes terrified people, and knowing what effective warriors we had become only scared them more. It also scared Adrien. He had no idea if we were stronger, and it drove him mad. Because of that, he tried to establish dominance over me and our people, causing great problems to develop between our communities. The day Adrien sent a group of guardsmen to us Alaric made his final mistake..."

ALEXANDER WOKE up when young Elysia ran in and jumped on the bed to rouse her parents. "Oh! Good morning, little girl. Why are you up so early?"

"I wanna go wif you to meet your Arcadians today. I'm big girl, and I can do it," Elysia had said.

He laughed at his toddler's fearlessness, adoring the quality in her. He found himself hoping it never changed.

"You know, I bet you could. In fact, I know you could, but today is a little different. Your mother says I need to delegate duties. She says I take too many responsibilities onto myself. It makes for less time to spend with both of you."

Elysia leaned in close, looking at her mother—who was pretending to be asleep—and then back at her father. "Mama doesn't know everything, Papa," she whispered.

The Chieftain put a single finger to his lips and whispered, "Shh... Don't tell her that. She thinks she does."

"That's because I do," she said, rolling over and giving away her wakefulness. "Elysia, you can't go with your father to meet the Arcadians today because he's sending Alaric to do it. That'll be Alaric's job from now on. Your father will be staying here where he's needed most, and he will train the children in magic while I train the warriors."

Elysia did not seem happy. "Fine. But dat not fair."

Alexander laughed and set her to the side, kissing her forehead. "I have a feeling, child, that there will be a great many things in your lifetime you feel are not fair. Consider this training."

He stood and made his way outside to find Alaric before he set out for the Forest border. He found him loading up the carriage he had hitched to the back of his horse. It was filled with wood that had been grown specifically to provide needed resources to Arcadia.

The druids had spent time creating a patch of land where they grew only Arcadian resources. Adrien wanted more and more all the time, but the Chieftain refused to give him more than he already had. The quantity had been agreed upon, and the Chieftain refused to give more. Arcadia traded clothing, bread, and bed linens for the wood.

"Let me know if things get worse. I fear our trading partnership with Adrien is ending. That path we've created from our home to the edge of the Forest may need to be grown over soon if he doesn't relent," Alexander said.

Alaric nodded. "I agree. He doesn't deserve anything from us. You know what I think we should do."

Alexander sighed. "Yes, I know what you and Jerick would like to see happen, but we aren't murderers. If and when Adrien poses a direct threat to our home or to our lives, we will engage in battle with him, but until then I have no interest in seeking war with someone I used to call a friend. There will be no violence."

Alaric snorted, shaking his head as he mumbled something about Alexander being weak.

Alexander ignored it, having come to expect that sort of behavior from him. "No violence. Is that understood?"

"Yes! I've got it," Alaric snapped.

Without another word, Alaric mounted his horse and urged him forward. Five other druids joined him on their own horses, two of them towing wagons full of wood.

It didn't take long for them to reach the border, and the Arcadians were already waiting. Something was different, though. Something was wrong.

They had no wagons with them.

Alaric dismounted, and the others followed suit. They approached the Arcadians. "Uh, good morning," Alaric said, eyeing them suspiciously. "What is this? Clearly, we've held up our end of the bargain. Where are your goods?"

One of the Arcadians stepped from the line, separating himself from the rest as leader. "Adrien says it's time to renegotiate. Where's Alexander?"

Alaric snorted again, just as he had earlier with Alexander. "Renegotiate? I don't think so. The deal was struck, and the deal will stand. Alexander isn't here. I am second in command. If you want to renegotiate, you'll do it with me, and I won't."

The Arcadian shook his head, chewing on his lower lip in irritation as he turned only his head to look back at his men. "Adrien demands that we be allowed into the Forest. What you're sending us isn't nearly enough to build an entire city. It's barely enough to build a bed, let alone a house for a full family plus furnishings. He wants Arcadian loggers to have full access. You can regrow everything. It shouldn't be a problem, right?"

"Wrong. Are you fucking serious? Why should we have to work because you bastards chose the wrong kind of magic to practice?" Alaric said snidely.

"We didn't come here to fight. We came here to strike a new deal. If there isn't one to be struck, we'll return to Adrien and tell him so. However, I can't say he will be happy about this. Are you sure you don't want to get Alexander? Perhaps he might be a bit more..." the Arcadian paused for a moment, "understanding."

"I'm in charge here. Alexander won't be agreeing to shit."

The Guard gave a deep sigh before nodding once. "Suit yourself, but don't say I didn't warn you or give you the opportunity for diplomacy." As the man made his way back to his horse, he muttered the words "fucking idiot" under his breath.

Unfortunately for him, he never stood a chance.

Before anyone could see what was happening, Alaric unsheathed his knife and sank it deep into his neck. The man fell to the ground, blood gurgling from the wound as he choked to death on his own essence.

The other guards realized what had happened and looked at Alaric with pure fury. One of them charged him, but Alaric easily dodged his attack and wrapped his hand around the man's neck.

The Arcadian began gasping for air as Alaric's eyes turned green, the very faintest of gray around his pupils. The others could feel the magic emanating from him, which made them feel cold. They could only watch in stunned silence as he used what he called the "death touch" on the second guard.

He had gotten better at it, and had learned not to use much since it would drain him quickly. He used only enough to make the man realize he was going to die before kicking his feet out from under him and snapping his neck with his strong hands.

He looked at the other guards with wild, murderous eyes, and they ran for their horses, riding out as fast as they could.

Alaric turned to his fellow warriors, his irises fading back to normal as his gaze locked on theirs. They stared at him with horror. "What?"

Emory, next in command after Alaric, shook his head. "How could you do that? You heard Alexander. No violence. You killed two of them. Do you have any idea what that means?"

Alaric laughed. "Hell yes, I do. It means they'll know who the fuck they're messing with. They'll know not to fuck with the Dark Forest. They'll also know not to question me again."

Emory's brows creased as his eyes narrowed. "Who are you? You didn't use to be like this. Can't you see what you've done? You didn't teach anyone a lesson—you just declared war. That man did not threaten you. He offered you a chance to get Alexander, which we should have taken. Alexander would've found a diplomatic way out of the situation without anyone losing their lives. He's not going to like this."

Alaric gave him a condescending smile. "Oh, he's not going to find out."

Confused, Emory looked at his fellow warriors, each of them sharing the same expression. "You're joking, right? He has to be told. Not only did you just kill two messengers, you are out of your mind. You're obsessed with power, just like Adrien. We heard him call you an idiot. Did we react? No. We stood behind you while you told him you were in charge, which made us look just as idiotic as you in his eyes. He called all of us that. We let it go because it's just a word. You killed two men who might have been perfectly innocent."

George, another warrior, nodded. "He's right. For all you know, this could've been their first week on the job. I've sure as hell not seen them before during the other shipment swaps. Adrien might have told them he's given us everything in the world, but we wouldn't cooperate with them. They could be innocent men, and you just killed them for no reason other than your pride."

Alaric nodded his head, feigning interest for a moment before he thrust his hand forward, vines bursting through the ground and wrapping around the throats of both Emory and George. Their eyes flashed green to defend themselves, but Alaric simply squeezed his hand, the vines tightening and snapping their necks.

"Who else thinks Alexander needs to know what really happened?" Alaric asked, taking a step toward the final three. Each of them shook his head, and he smiled. "Good! Glad to hear it. Now, let's get our good friends into the carts. It's a shame the Arcadians killed them."

The remaining three warriors nodded as each of them muttered unevenly, "Yeah, that's a shame."

To make sure it was a believable story, Alaric used his knife to stab George in the throat, letting the blood soak his neck to hide the bruises left by the vines. He took a sword from one of the dead guards and took Emory's head off for the same reason.

Once that was finished, the bodies were loaded and taken to the village. Alaric told the whole story while the other three stood silently nodding behind him. Alexander could sense that something was off. He felt something cold and dead, and it wasn't the bodies in the carts.

He knew Alaric had used that magic. The death touch.

His people had used it while hunting, and he himself had once used it to ease the passing of an Elder. Each time it had been used, there was a sense of purity that accompanied it—except right then, and the first time Alexander had sensed Alaric using it. There seemed to be a dark correlation between Alaric and that power that no other druid was capable of.

At that moment, Alexander realized it was the intention behind the use that caused the foulness. It came from the soul of the person calling it. Alexander and his people used that magic only in times when it was truly needed, as a form of mercy.

Alaric used it just because he could.

"You would stand here and lie to my face?" Alexander asked. "After all we've been through? You would choose power over friendship? You would choose power and control over loyalty and love?"

Alaric's face fell as he sighed. Then he shrugged, bursting into laughter. "You know, if you didn't believe me, you could've just told me so. I'm sick and tired of hiding. I'm sick and tired of faking who I am. You seem to think I'm some dark, evil monster. That couldn't be further from the truth. If anyone here is dark and evil, it's you."

Alexander's eyes widened. "Me? How can you say such a thing? I've made mistakes just like anyone else, but my heart has always been in the right place. I've never wanted anything but a peaceful home and healthy people. Food. Shelter. Love. Basic necessities for any human being. You crave more and more of anything that you are handed."

Rolling his eyes, Alaric said, "See? That's exactly the shit I'm talking about. You seem to think the world is all about roses and what-the-fuck-ever else. It isn't. The Arcadians are demanding access to the Dark Forest. They want to put loggers in here to cut it all down. Our home! What would you do? Oh, wait—don't even bother answering. I know exactly what you would do. You'd roll over and let them do it. You don't have what I have. You're pathetic. I'm the only one fit to rule over this community."

Alexander shook his head. "We didn't come so far and achieve so much just for us to lose everything we've worked for. I would never let anyone take our home from us. We will work day and night to create a barrier strong enough to keep them out. Nothing and no one will be able to get past it if they aren't one of us."

Alaric smiled. "Well, look at you! There's something. Let's get to work on that."

Alexander shook his head. "Oh, we will, but you will have no part in it. You no longer have a place in the Dark Forest. You don't belong here anymore. I've allowed you to get away with far too much. I took you away from training children because I thought you just weren't very good with them, but it turned out you were tormenting them. Children! And now you're a murderer. You have a lust for power, and I have no doubt in my mind that if I turned my back at the wrong time—if I did even one thing you didn't approve of—you would take my life as well."

"You're damn right I would! If you were too weak to do what needed to be done, I would. And yes, I would kill you if it meant being strong enough for our people. You should be grateful for what I did. You should be grateful for the way I treated the children. They will grow up stronger for it. You should be grateful for everything I've done that you couldn't. Hell, you and everyone else should kneel at my feet."

Alexander couldn't believe the words coming from Alaric's mouth. He couldn't believe how far his friend had fallen. He'd had some idea, but he hadn't completely understood until then. He loved Alaric, so he hadn't been able to face the truth before.

But he could now.

"Alaric, leave now, or you will be forcibly removed," Alexander said firmly, his fists clenched at his sides. Several warriors stepped forward, ready to defend Alexander and their people if necessary, each of them having heard the words Alaric had spoken as a threat.

Alaric smiled. "If you think for an instant I'm the only one who thinks this way, you're dead wrong. You will regret this. We'll see each other again, old friend, and when we do, my death touch will completely drain the life from you. I won't stop until you and anyone standing behind you—including that little brat of yours—either kneels at my feet or dies by my hands."

THE CHIEFTAIN LOOKED AROUND at his captivated audience and Zoe slowly pulled her hands back. Everyone seemed to be as taken aback by what had happened with Alaric as Alexander had been that morning. Elysia was most affected, now knowing her life had been threatened when she was a toddler.

"As you can imagine, Alaric was escorted out of the Dark Forest. That night, we worked together—men, women, and children—until we had the barrier started. Every night after that, we each took to the barrier and grew it taller, thicker, and stronger. It took weeks, but once it was established it was easy for us to build outwards. As our community grew, we made it bigger.

"ALARIC'S BROTHER, Jerick, left soon after, and several others with him. I didn't ask questions, just allowed them to go. It was their choice. After that, we focused on ourselves. We cut off all deliveries to and from Arcadia, and we very much became the threat the city had believed us to be. Not even Adrien dared to mess with us once the barrier was erected. He knew better."

The Chieftain finished the rest of his wine before setting his mug down. "After that day, everyone was in awe that I had put the community before myself, even casting away someone who had been very important to me to protect our people. It was because of that very day that everyone began calling me 'Chieftain,' and not sarcastically, as Alaric had done. Over the years, we've had several run-ins with Alaric and his people, but we never truly had the threat of war. Until now."

"We're not going to let them take the Forest. You didn't let them take it back then, and we're not going to let them take it now," Arryn said, her face full of defiance and fury.

Several people raised their mugs, everyone else following suit shortly after. "*For the Dark Forest!*"

The Chieftain smiled a bit sadly. He raised what was left of his mug of strong wine. "For the Forest."

He drank the rest of it before setting the mug on his chair and excusing himself, as he had each night that he forced himself to relive that terrible past.

CHAPTER TEN

Aeris usually walked alongside his Chieftain at the front of the line since they were the strongest in the tribe, but today was different. It had been different ever since they had left the Terres Forest. Alaric's brother, Jerick, was his righthand man now, and as such stood in the position Aeris had held dear.

Aeris had more or less been thrown to the side.

It didn't matter to him that Jerick was Alaric's brother. They'd been feuding for *years*, and Aeris had been by his side for a decade. Dedicated his life and purpose to him as well as his vision.

Now cast away, he realized exactly how expendable he was in comparison to the Chieftain's brother.

But then again, Aeris hadn't *always* been there.

Aeris had been Alaric's enemy for quite some time before he had come to realize just how unevenly the Chieftain of the Dark Forest operated. How he picked and chose his favorites, breaking the rules for them while enforcing them with others.

Arryn...

A child in danger...

Her age shouldn't have mattered, or that she was in danger.

Arryn was an Arcadian—an outsider. That meant she was the child of an enemy. Aeris couldn't see it then, and he still couldn't see why in Irth the Chieftain broke the rules for such a spoiled brat.

Especially given that Adrien might have come searching for her.

Perhaps he would get to ask Alexander that question himself one day very soon. Maybe he would find out exactly why he had risked the lives of his people over some noble whelp from the city.

Of course, after overhearing some of the conversations Alaric had recently had with Jerick, Aeris was no longer convinced his own Chieftain was very different from the one he had abandoned.

It seemed Alaric would be just as ready as Alexander to sacrifice his people under the right circumstances.

Those circumstances being taking the Dark Forest, of course.

Aeris didn't plan to just sit around and wait for the moment Alaric decided he was no longer good enough to remain by his side. He wouldn't allow himself to be disgraced again—to be taken for granted.

And he wouldn't allow that to happen to Jenna either.

Poor Jenna...

When he left she had been stuck in the Dark Forest with people who were cold and judgmental, and he knew she had suffered a great deal.

While it was true that she had become a warrior, he had a feeling Alexander had put her in that place to prove a point. Surely it wasn't because he actually trusted her, as he had told her. He had always wondered if it'd had more to do with proving he was in control—that the Chieftain wasn't afraid of someone like Aeris or Alaric.

She'd had to force herself to train with them, fight for them and alongside them, while they silently judged her for sins that were not her own. While Jenna herself still believed the Chieftain of the Dark Forest had once placed faith in her, Aeris knew better. That lesson had taken a long time to learn.

No one could be trusted.

Only family.

He and Jenna were all that was left. All he had. His parents had stuck around with them when they had been liberated, but they had still believed in Alexander—though they were smart enough not to say such a thing, so they could stay with their children, no matter what the cost.

Still, Aeris believed from the bottom of his heart that his parents would have turned on him and Jenna in a heartbeat if it had meant with absolute certainty they could get back into Alexander's good graces.

Jenna might have her flaws, but she truly was all he had in the world. He planned to see to it that neither of them ever had to fear or worry about anything else as long as they lived.

Over the past hour, Aeris had gradually decreased his pace, allowing the dark druids to pass him and slowly dropping back so it didn't seem suspicious. His place had always been in the front, as next in line for power, and since Jenna was third in line, she always took the rear.

Her death touch was strong like Alaric's. Her dark magic had been acquired much faster than her pure nature magic ever had. It had more or less made her the Chieftain's second adopted child, which had pleased Aeris.

Perhaps she had been meant to be a dark druid all along. It was where her powers were the strongest.

"Is everything okay?" Jenna asked, knowing it was unusual to see her brother at the rear.

He nodded and said quietly, "I wanted to speak to you alone."

That certainly caught her attention. "All right. What's going on?"

He paused as he judged the distance between them and the

rest of the druids ahead of them. "I know you came here to get away. I also know you wanted to support me and even Alaric, but things have changed."

Jenna's eyes narrowed a bit as she searched his expression, though she could only see it from a side angle. "Of course, I support you. I'll ask you one more time: what's going on, Aeris? What's changed?"

There was a pause before he continued, "I don't think Alaric has our best interests at heart. I truly believe he would send every one of us against Alexander, even if he knew it meant certain death."

Jenna kept her expression as level as possible as she nodded. "Do you have a plan to do something about this, or are you just planning to wing it?"

"I have a plan, but I'm going to need your help. It involves Arryn," he said, turning his eyes toward his sister's as they continued to walk behind the crowd. "You're absolutely sure she's powerful?"

Jenna almost laughed. "Oh, I'm positive. You didn't see the level of magic she used in the *Versuch*. It wasn't allowed, but she got away with it like she gets away with *everything*. I'm sure by now she's learned how to control her abilities better, too. If she has, she's probably strong enough to take down Alaric on her own."

Aeris thought about his sister's words carefully. He couldn't quite guarantee his idea would work, but if everything went according to plan, he certainly stood a good chance.

"Years ago, shortly after Arryn arrived, I went after her father, Christopher. He was still alive, and I took him because I knew one day he would be useful. I didn't care about anything else—not power, not control of the Dark Forest, none of that. I just wanted to kill Arryn. I didn't give a fuck if she was ten or a hundred and ten. She deserves to die, and her father deserves worse."

"I know all that," Jenna said. "The question is, what exactly do you plan to do with him?"

He smiled. "I'm going to lure Arryn out of the Dark Forest, and I'm going to use Christopher to do it. If we can get Arryn here with us, maybe I can use her to kill both Chieftains. Once they're dead, the people *will* follow me. There are several who put as little trust in him as I do. They want new leadership, and we can give that to them. They know we would respect them. We wouldn't throw wave after wave of them at Alexander just to watch them die like Alaric would."

Jenna smiled. "No. We'll formulate a foolproof plan that will win us our prize. We have supplies in the cave. Parchment and ink. I know I brought some with me when I first came, but I think others stole some as well. I'm betting Arryn will remember Daddy Dearest's signature. Maybe we should have him send a letter."

Aeris had to control his excitement as he realized just how easily everything would fall into place. "We're close enough now that if we sent a bird ahead to Jace, he could get the letter written and sent off by the time we got back home. Within a day or two, that bitch would find her way to us."

"What if she shows the letter to Alexander? Wouldn't he convince her it was a setup?"

He shrugged. "I'm going to make sure we have backup. I plan to tell the Chieftain about this. If he knows we intend to separate Arryn, he'll believe it's to make the druids of the Dark Forest weaker. In reality, we'll seal his fate. If Arryn comes to us, fantastic. If Alexander convinces her it's a trap, it won't matter because we'll be on our way to get her. My hope is that we'll meet her in the middle and avoid confrontation with the others altogether. We will burn the leaves and use the wind to fan it through the barrier toward the villages."

Jenna nodded. "We can send men to the southern side of the border as well as the eastern side. With that smoke blowing in from both directions, there will be nowhere to run. The problem is, Alaric will want to take the Dark Forest right then if we convince him we're ready to attack and remove Arryn."

"Leave Alaric to me. I'll be able to compel him not to attack before we get Arryn. I'll use his paranoia and ego against him." He sighed as he smiled. "No one will be able to stop us. We get in, take Arryn, and get her back to the south end of the Forest. When she sees her father, she'll see exactly how far off he is—how crazy he's become—and she'll lose her mind."

Aeris laughed with excitement, realizing just how close they were to having a full strategy. "And if she's as strong as you say she is, she'll rip that place apart to get to Alaric and Jerick. She will think it was all them, and she'll do the hard work for us."

"That's brilliant," Jenna said. "Why don't you find your messenger? If anyone asks, I'll tell them you went to take a leak."

Aeris smiled again and nodded once before looking around to make sure no one was watching. Once he was satisfied all eyes were on the road ahead, he ran toward the edge of the woods to call a fast bird he could use to send his message.

IT HAD TAKEN two days of travel, but Bast, Cleo, and the rearick all made the trip safely to Arcadia. When they arrived, the guards at the gate stopped all of them, as was usual.

Adam, one of the guards, stepped forward and smiled. "Hey, Sven! It's good to see you. Who are your friends here? I haven't seen them before."

Sven jerked his head in their direction. "These lassies right here saved our arses on the road from Craigston. Had it not been fer them, we'd 've been dead fer sure. In fact, that 'un right there leanin' over a bit, she damn near kicked the bucket. She needs medical attention, but she's stable all right. Stitched 'er up meself."

The guard's expression turned serious then, concern spreading across his face as he looked at Cleo. He nodded once. "I'll escort her to the medical building right away." He turned to Bast. "Ma'am, you're more than welcome to come with us. You're both safe now. No harm will come to you here as long as you mean no harm to anyone else."

Bast looked at her wounded sister. Cleo slumped over her horse a bit, but she was alive. A bit of hope lit her eyes, matching Bast's. Not only had they made it to Arcadia, but the first person they had met was a kind and gentle soul.

"Thank you," Bast said. "She took a sword across her chest. Sven stitched her, but I know she could use some herbs and proper cleaning."

He nodded before motioning to his fellow guards. They quickly ran over, and he gave them orders to take his place and find another to replace him. He walked them inside, stopping at the Guard post to get a horse for himself before leading the way through the city.

Bast and Cleo admired the large, beautiful trees that graced the main street. Some of the buildings looked like they had recently taken damage, and there were men and women working on a couple of them. Stones were being lifted and put into place with telekinesis, while on others, people were using wood to fix some of the walls.

It was a sight to see. Magic everywhere, just like they had been told.

"Once you get us settled, would it be possible for us to speak to a woman named Amelia? Do you know her?" Bast asked.

Adam nodded. "I do. She's our governor. If you wish to speak to her, I'll bring her the message. The medical building isn't far from the Capitol building. May I ask what it's regarding?"

"I'm sure you can tell by looking at us that we aren't from around here," Bast said, referring to her creamy, mocha-toned skin and obsidian hair.

Normally, it was very kinky and curly, but she had straightened it to more easily put it in a single long braid for fighting. Cleo liked to wear hers in thin, tight box-braids and tie all of them together. Both girls had emerald-green, catlike eyes, and they wore eyeliner to accentuate their beautiful, dramatic features.

Their look was customary where they were from, but very unique in a place like Arcadia. People stopped to look at them with genuine interest and what appeared to be awe as they made their way through the city.

Bast smiled at a little girl who flashed her a big toothless grin. "We traveled for two weeks from our homeland to get to the Temple, where we were told by a mystic there to come see a woman named Amelia in Arcadia. They said she might be able to help."

Adam nodded. "I don't know exactly what you need help with, but if anyone can help you it's Amelia. Though… I don't know if the mystics told you or not, but we have been through hell over the last year. A lot of things have happened here, and Amelia went to the deepest circle to pull us out. While I hope your journey here wasn't for nothing, I want you to keep that in mind."

They finally arrived, cutting the conversation off temporarily. Adam helped Bast get her twin sister inside and seated on a medical table.

Cleo grunted as she got herself in a comfortable position, at least as much as was possible. "Margit didn't elaborate, but she did mention the city having had a hard time as of late. I'm sorry to hear that. Even if she can't directly help, if she can point us in the direction of someone who can, I would be very grateful."

"The two of ye need ta get some rest, is what ye need," Sven said from behind them.

Bast and Cleo both smiled, though the rearick couldn't see it.

Adam nodded as two women came into the room to sit next to Cleo. "Very well, then. I'll be back within the hour to give you an update, though I can't promise when Amelia might arrive. She's still very busy, but that doesn't necessarily mean anything. She's very kind, and I'm sure she'll make time for you quickly."

Bast and Cleo both gave nods of thanks as he turned and left the medical building. Cleo groaned deep in her throat as the second woman began cutting her shirt off.

The woman grimaced as she looked at the wound. "Child, this looks terrible. It stretches all the way from your left shoulder to under your rib cage on the right. I don't know how you survived this."

Cleo snorted. "It's not as deep as it looks, but it sure as hell hurts like it was. If I hadn't dodged, I'd be a little less alive today. The Bitch has blessed me with speed."

The caretaker nodded, giving her a smile. "She certainly has. My name is Clarice. I'm the doctor here, and this is my assistant, Sherry."

Cleo nodded at both, and ground her teeth as Clarice began poking and prodding her wound. She saw the woman grimace again. "That's not the expression of someone who's happy about what she sees."

Clarice sighed as she sat back. "Unfortunately, you're right. About a few things, actually. First, while the wound isn't as deep as it looks, in a couple places it went down to the bone. Deep or not, I don't know how you survived this. Secondly, your friend obviously did an excellent job of keeping you alive. I would have to say that if not for him, you wouldn't have made it here alive, much less in good humor. That being said, the wound wasn't properly cleaned, and I see signs of infection beginning."

Cleo swallowed hard, knowing what that meant. She took a deep breath and blew it out, nodding. "Knock my ass out *hard*. I don't even wanna know I'm alive."

"I take it you know what comes next?" Clarice asked.

Both Cleo and Bast nodded. Bast looked at her sister with compassion before turning her gaze to Clarice. "Where we come from, girls didn't used to train to fight. That slowly began to change, and now they'll take able-bodied fighters no matter their gender. But back then, our mom just wanted us to be innocent little girls. We didn't care much for that."

Both girls laughed, Cleo immediately regretting the decision as she tensed up with pain.

"One day, we got our father's swords and began training with them. We were twelve at the time. Cleo came at me and sliced my thigh open almost from hip to knee. It wasn't very deep, about like that one right there, but we had to hide what had happened."

Cleo nodded, continuing her sister's story. "I ran and got the towels and the needle and thread. It was my job to slow the bleeding while she stitched it up. She did a terrible job, but it worked."

"Until a few days later, when it festered. I got a fever, and we had no choice but to tell Mama what happened. She had to use a hot wet towel to soften the scab and scrape it all off, then open the wound again and clean it with soap, hot water, and antiseptic. That's a pain I will *never* forget," Bast finished.

With a sigh, Cleo said, "I remember just how loud she screamed and how she damn near broke my hand. So, like I said —I want you to knock my ass out. I don't even wanna know I'm alive."

The doctor nodded. "Unfortunately, that's very true. Not only because that's what I'm gonna have to do, but also because this will probably be far more painful. It's on the chest, and you don't have nearly the amount of meat there that a thigh does. I'm out of some of my supplies because of everything that has happened recently. It'll take me a couple hours, but I can hunt down some belladonna and make you a tea."

Cleo shook her head. "That'll take too long. Now that I know you have to pull the stitches out, pull this apart, scrape it clean, wash it, and sterilize it, my adrenaline is going. I'm ready now. If you wait, I'll freak myself out. Either hit me with something, or get me some strong alcohol."

Bast shrugged as the doctor looked at her. While the doctor was concerned, Bast wasn't. She knew her sister, and knew she was very serious.

Sven came in holding a jug, and Cleo shook her head. "I'd rather be wide-awake while she does this than drink that shit again. That's probably what made it rot to begin with."

The rearick smiled and shook his head. "Hey, rearick brew ain't all that bad. It prolly kept the rot *away*, young lassie. But this ain't that swill, so don't you worry. I went down ta the bar, antici-patin' this might be painful fer ye, and she gave me what was left in this jug. It ain't a lot, but it should do."

Cleo held out her hand, immediately pulling the jug to her mouth and chugging some of it. It burned terribly, but it wasn't nearly as bad as whatever Sven had given her on the road.

In half an hour, Cleo was completely drunk, thanks to the empty stomach she'd had when she began drinking, and Doctor Clarice began removing the stitches. The girl held it together for a while, until the doctor began peeling away the scab she had softened with a hot towel.

They put a dry rag in her mouth as she screamed, but it didn't do much good. She spat it out, shrieking, "*Ah! Fucking Bitch and Bastard*!" before launching into a series of creative and admittedly comical oaths no one in the room—even her sister—had heard before.

Bast had to turn her head to keep from laughing, knowing just how painful the procedure was from her own personal experience.

"Get that rearick sonofabitch in here!" Cleo shouted. "Have 'im punch me in the face!"

Brighter light shined in through the door as it opened, and a beautiful woman stepped through it with confusion and worry on her face. "What the hell's going on in here?"

Cleo lifted only her eyes, her chin still on her chest as she scowled at whoever had come in. "Who the fuck is that, now? It sure as shit ain't the rearick!" She screamed again, throwing her head back.

"Amelia," the doctor said, a bit of relief in her voice. "Cleo here came in with the group of rearick. They said she and her sister saved their lives. I'm trying to clean her wound, but it isn't going well."

Amelia's eyes widened as she stepped farther in and saw the half-naked girl lying on the table with her chest cut open. "Sonofabitch," Amelia said. "Why the hell didn't you knock her out?"

"Gah! *Thank you*," Cleo groaned out. "I'd like to know the *same* fucking thing."

"Wait, you're Amelia?" Bast asked.

"Ouch, motherfucker," Cleo said. "What part of Clarice calling her 'Amelia' didn't give that away?"

Bast snorted. "Boy, you sure are mean when you're in a little pain."

If looks could kill, Bast would have died with a thousand knives piercing her face right then. Cleo glared the daggers at her instead before grimacing with another round of pain.

"*Clarice*," Amelia said sternly, "anesthesia. Why isn't there any?"

Clarice sighed. "With everything that happened with the mystics, I'm out of drugs. I offered to find belladonna, but she said no. We gave her enough whiskey to take down a grown-ass rearick. She's all of ninety-five pounds, and she drank enough to kill a man twice that. She should've been unconscious by now."

Bast thought she saw the hint of a smile on Amelia's face as she came to stand at the foot of the table, but a concerned expression replaced it.

"I don't know if I'll be able to help, but I'll give it a shot," Amelia said as she pushed back Cleo's pants legs to reveal her bare ankles. She wrapped her hands around them, her eyes flashing white as she did.

Within seconds Cleo's pain-filled expression faded. Her body was almost relaxed.

Amelia nodded. "I'm not as good as a real mystic, not by a longshot. We don't have much time, so get moving. She'll still feel pain, but hopefully it won't be nearly as bad. I don't have the power to knock her out."

No one spoke as Clarice once again began cleaning the wound. She moved as quickly as possible, using a new hot, wet rag to wipe away what little scabbing had occurred on the surface along with the pus.

As she was switching rags, readying the next step, the girl passed out. Having Amelia calming her and helping her deal with the pain had allowed her enough comfort to be able to fall asleep, and she had succumbed to the effects of the alcohol.

It was a miracle, one they were each grateful for.

Though Amelia didn't have to use her power much after that, she stuck around in case Cleo woke up. It took over an hour, but the wound was cleaned and re-stitched. From there, they would just have to clean it carefully and re-wrap it properly every day.

Several hours later Cleo finally awoke, her head splitting from the hangover. She groaned as Bast handed her a mug. "Drink this. I've had it ready for you, since I figured you'd wake up with a nasty headache."

Without speaking, Cleo took the mug and drank it all down before handing it back to her sister. She sighed heavily and laid back, lifting her hands to massage her head.

"That was seriously the worst pain I think I have ever felt in my life."

Bast smiled. "Before this is over, I have a feeling you'll be saying that again about something else."

Cleo knew her sister was referring to the fight back home. She gasped, her eyes widening and her hands falling to her sides as she turned to her sister. "Amelia! We need to talk to her!"

A soft shushing sound came from across the room. It was

Amelia. Cleo had thought she had left. "Don't worry about all that right now. I know that's easier said than done, but do your best. Focus on yourself. Bast already told me everything."

Cleo looked at her sister again, obvious questions floating in her mind.

"Amelia says she is stuck here because of her duty to her own people, but she knows a group of people who would probably be willing to help," Bast said.

Amelia nodded. "Unfortunately, the druids of the Dark Forest are about to fight a war of their own. I have a friend there whose name is Arryn. The two of you should stay here in Arcadia where it's safe until that fight is over. It shouldn't be long now."

"Wait, they have to go to war too? Didn't you just have a war *here*? What the *hell* is going on in this valley?" Cleo asked as she looked from Amelia to Bast and back.

Her sister smiled, smoothing back the dampened braids that had fallen around Cleo's face. "It really *is* a long story. Arcadia's problems have been settled, but now the druids must fight for their home. They helped take Arcadia back from darkness, and now they have to fight for their own people and for their own home."

Cleo's brows furrowed. "Fuck that."

Both Bast and Amelia's eyes widened. Bast leaned closer to her sister. "Cleo, if there's anyone in this world who understands what they're going through, it's us. How can you say that?"

Shaking her head, Cleo said, "No. I *do* understand. That's why we're not gonna sit here on our asses while they fight for their lives. How's that going to sound? 'Hey, we knew you had a war to fight, but we kind of hung out in the safe city and let you do that by yourself when we *totally* had the strength to help. We didn't do shit for you, but how would you like to come back with us and help us fight our battle?'"

Bast nodded. "Okay, I see your point. So… what? Do you think you're in any condition to fight? I agree we should help them with their fight if we plan to ask them for help with ours, but we also can't just run out there with you in so much pain. You could bust your stitches open. You could be slow enough that someone could kill you."

"Hmmm..." Amelia drawled. "I don't mean to get in the middle of this, but the druids have different magic than what you've probably ever heard of. They can heal, among many other things. Bast, earlier when we were talking, you mentioned the trees in the street. Those were grown in just a couple of minutes by several druids. All they have to do is touch your sister, and that wound would be gone in seconds."

Cleo smiled. "See? It's meant to be. We were meant to come here, especially right now. We can help them win their fight, and my injury won't even matter."

Bast seemed a bit more excited about the idea. "Once they heal you, we'll be ready to fight by their sides."

Amelia smiled. "I'm sad I'm going to miss out on this one."

CHAPTER ELEVEN

Arryn and Corrine once again woke early, before the sun had even risen. The Chieftain had resumed regular festivities the night before, which Arryn suspected was because he'd had such a hard time talking about the past. Most of his tale had been told, although he had skimmed over many years to keep his nightly storytelling sessions on that particular subject as short as possible.

The important parts had been told. She understood now, and so did everyone else.

High in the trees the birds were singing loudly, like they always did first thing in the morning—a sound that Arryn could never get enough of. As they walked, Corrine reached out and grabbed her hand. Arryn smiled and gave it a hard squeeze and twined their fingers as they continued to walk.

"Can I ask you a question?" Corrine asked.

Arryn smiled. "You just did, but yes."

"I know you probably don't like to think about it, but I heard you talking to Celine a few days ago about your father. You said the dark druids have him. Are you sure?"

"I'm not sure about anything. There's no way for me to know

if they have him or not, but I suspect they do. At the very least, they *did.* After all this time, they might have killed him, but several things tell me he's still alive," Arryn answered.

Corrine kicked a small rock out of her path, pulling Arryn forward a bit as she did. "Well, what things tell you that?"

Arryn shrugged. "It's not proof or anything, but my gut tells me he's alive. Deep down, I just feel like that's the truth. Other than that, about two months ago I was dumped on the top of the tallest mountain in the Frozen North. While I was there, the dark druids attacked the southern village to take back one of their own.

"A mystic named Scarlett was with them, helping them. When I heard the story, I couldn't understand why she'd do that, except that she'd planned to use them in return. The day I killed her, she talked about my father. She mentioned telling him something about how terrible I was—I don't really remember. But she talked about him in the present tense, as if she knew where he was and that he was alive."

Corrine looked up as a chubby squirrel loudly chased another through the branches. "Do you believe her?"

Arryn laughed. "You sure are full of questions this morning. Zoe told me Scarlett didn't know where he was, but I suspect otherwise. Elon told us someone with what sounded suspiciously like dark druid abilities snuck into the city and took him. That tells me they have him now. Given Scarlett had helped them and had later mentioned him as she did, I think she might have even seen him. None of that is proof, of course, but I believe it."

"Why haven't you gone after him?" she asked. "I'll help you find him!"

Arryn lifted Corrine's little hand to her mouth, kissing the back of it. "You are a very sweet girl, but there is still so much for you to learn. You have lost so much, and so have I. Let's not lose each other, okay? Because if I go alone, I won't make it back. If you go, neither will you. Even together, we wouldn't survive. It would take much more than that."

She sighed as she looked down into eyes that had seen so much, yet still looked at her with absolute trust—a trust she hadn't ever experienced in her short life.

"We have to wait until the time is right, and I have to believe the Chieftain and Elysia. I keep reminding myself that they've never led me astray. If the dark druids have kept him alive this long, they're not going to kill him anytime soon."

As they approached the training pit, they saw Samuel and Celine already out there practicing. They had spent a lot of time on ranged weapons, and now he was teaching her hand-to-hand combat. He wanted to show her the rearick way, because it was quicker to learn and very practical in a pinch. He decided that once she knew how to properly throw a punch, she could learn the "fancy footwork," as he called it, if she wanted. She would have a great foundation.

"What if they're hurting him?" Corrine asked.

Arryn stopped, a heavy sigh escaping her. "I know that's more than likely the situation, but I can't let myself focus on that. You have no idea how hard it is for me to stand around here knowing that could be happening, but the truth is, if I run off, I don't just risk my own life.

"If I die, what happens to Cathillian? I know how much he cares about me, and he might do something without thinking first. What if he died? What would happen to his mother? To his grandfather? If anything happened to them, what would happen to the tribe?

"I would never think I'm important enough to determine the tribe's future, but I *do* know how important family is. They love me, and I love them. Family means everything here, and if something happened to me, it *would* hurt them. That's not a risk I'm willing to take. That was what my father taught me the day he sent me here—those you love are more important than your own personal well-being. I just hope I can hold it together a little while longer, because just between the two of us, I'm about to lose it."

———

JACE HAD JUST FINISHED GATHERING what he could for breakfast when a falcon flew overhead. It landed on a stone at the mouth of the cave before flying over to land on a tree stump that was used for sitting around the fire pit.

The dark druid eyed him suspiciously when he saw the parchment wrapped around his leg. Jace, knowing he didn't have pure enough nature magic to communicate with animals, approached with caution.

The raptor twisted his head to the side as if waiting for him with impatience. Finally, Jace reached out and untied the string that held the parchment in place.

He knew it could have only come from the druids of the Dark Forest or from Aeris. Even Jenna lacked the ability to control animals any longer, at least not without using extreme force.

Unrolling it, his eyes wandered to the end and Aeris' signature.

Jace,

Ready the prisoner. Have him write a letter to his daughter that will get her attention. Make sure there's a sense of danger and urgency. We need to separate her from the rest. The falcon will wait for you to attach another note. Once you do, he will fly to the druids of the Dark Forest. Don't give him any further instructions. I've already compelled him.

—Aeris

Jace smiled as he looked at the cave. For ten years, he had been in charge of watching Christopher. Ten years he'd had the childish job of babysitting. Making sure the man was fed, making sure he was under control, and making sure he didn't run off.

Finally, he would be rid of that troublesome responsibility.

Because of Christopher he'd had to stay behind while the others went to the Terres Forest. He had been forced to take him and their other prisoner into the cave and through the tunnels deep enough that no one would know they were there.

Twice, people had come looking for the dark druids, but they hadn't been brave enough or stupid enough to travel that far into the darkness. He looked at the letter from Aeris, and then at his bowl of fruit. Some of the berries were only partially rotted, but he was quite excited about it. It was his best work yet.

Unlike those bastards in the Dark Forest, he didn't have the power to create healthy plants, but that wouldn't matter soon enough. The time was coming for them to take back the Dark Forest, and then they would have plenty of food to eat.

He groaned as his belly growled with the memory of what fresh berries tasted like.

He set the bowl down and stuffed a handful of gooey, partially rotted raspberries in his mouth. After wiping his hands off on his pants, he walked inside the cave, grabbed a bag, and removed a quill, ink, and parchment, placing them just in the light of the cave entrance.

After taking a torch that hung on the wall, he made his way through the tunnels to an open room that held two people. They looked up, shielding their eyes. Neither were in chains, because neither needed to be. Christopher was under the control of his teas and other things he concocted from various leaves or mushrooms that kept his mind cluttered.

The woman, Dana, had been at one time, but he weaned her off the teas out of loneliness. He knew she wouldn't run or attack him because she worried too much about her uncle.

Dana knew he would be killed if she did any such thing, so it allowed him someone to talk to from time to time—though she was never particularly fond of their conversations, she still complied.

"Christopher," Jace said, his voice echoing off the walls. "I need you to come with me. I have work for you."

Dana, who sat across from him, became visibly worried. "What's going on? Where are you taking him?"

Jace sighed and rolled his eyes. "I have been *very* kind to you. I've noticed that you stay put whether on or off the tea, and I know it's for him. I'm not taking him to hurt him, but let me be clear: if you try to leave or try to get in my way, I will put you back under. Is that understood?"

If Aeris had known Jace had taken Dana off the tea, he wouldn't have been happy. But if she wasn't in her right mind, who would he talk to?

Aeris hadn't given him that position out of trust and kindness, but because he didn't respect him. Worse…the Chieftain had agreed to it, which meant he didn't either. He'd been with Alaric from the beginning, and he believed he damned well deserved his respect.

Since he didn't have that, he had no problem making up his own rules as he went along. And he saw no reason to poison the girl if she was determined to stay.

Dana nodded. "Please, just be kind to him. I won't go anywhere or try anything."

Jace crossed the room and grabbed Christopher by the arm, lifting him off the ground. Christopher looked wildly around the room, muttering something about bugs and the fall of man.

The herbs Jace had put in his tea that morning had been particularly strong. He just hoped they had worn off enough that he could at least keep his head straight to write a letter.

The dark druid led him to the edge of the cave, sitting him down next to a stone that was flat enough to write on. He pointed to the parchment and inkwell before handing him the quill.

"Christopher, I need you to write a letter to your daughter. Do you remember your daughter?" Jace asked.

Christopher continued to shake his head as he looked around with paranoia, jerking every so often and wiping his filthy face with his even filthier hand.

"Hey!" Jace said, thwapping him on the back of the head. "Do you remember your daughter? Your little girl?"

When the crazed man didn't respond, Jace got on his knees and grabbed the man by the face, his eyes boring into Christopher's. He repeated his question.

Christopher stared at him for several moments, eyes darting back and forth as they shifted focus from one of Jace's eyes to the other. His mouth moved, and he muttered something, but Jace couldn't understand him.

"What?" Jace asked.

Christopher began to blink wildly as his eyes became unfocused. "Arryn." It was only a tiny bit louder, but enough for Jace to hear.

He remembered.

"Good! Yes, Arryn. Do you remember Arryn?"

Tears began to fill Christopher's eyes as his breathing increased. "Little girl. She's just little girl…"

"What if I told you I knew where she was?" Jace said with a smile. "I can get a letter to her."

Christopher's eyes all but lit up as tears spilled onto his cheeks. "Little Arryn? You know where she is? No." He began shaking his head violently. "No one can know. She *must* be safe. I *have* to keep her safe."

Jace grabbed Christopher's wrists, doing his best to keep his patience. "Arryn *is* safe. In fact, she's safer now than she ever has been, but that might change soon."

Christopher's eyes widened. "What? Is it Adrien? Has he found her? You must keep me safe. You have to keep Arryn safe!"

Jace nodded. "Bad people are coming for her, Christopher. She's not safe. I'll do my best, but if they can't find you they might find Arryn. Then she *won't* be safe. You need to write her a letter and tell her the danger she is in. Tell her so she'll come here to be with you."

Christopher shook his head. "No, she can't be harmed! Please help me. I have to get her here with us, where she can be safe."

It appeared the man's love for his daughter was sobering him faster than he had anticipated. "Telling her that *you're* the one in danger will get her to come here as quickly as possible. If you tell her that *she's* the one in danger, it might cause her to run in a different direction to try to save you both. We can't risk that, now can we? She *has* to come here."

Christopher mouthed the word "Oh" as he nodded. "That makes sense."

Jace nearly laughed, knowing that it in fact did *not* make sense, but that was for him to know.

"What should I put in the letter?" Christopher asked.

Jace smiled and said, "Just write exactly what I tell you. When she sees your handwriting and your signature, she'll come running."

CHAPTER TWELVE

Arryn had just finished sparring with Celine when she saw the Chieftain making his way toward the pit. Unless there was significant reason for it, he usually didn't visit there. His duties were magical training and being the class clown.

There must be something wrong or something that couldn't wait, especially given the look on his face. He stared down, and the bad feeling in her belly grew.

"Arryn, can I talk to you for a minute?" the Chieftain asked, his voice serious.

She looked at Celine for a moment, then handed her staff to her aunt and went to the Chieftain. "What's wrong?"

There was something in his hand, and he stared at it for several moments before extending it to her. She looked at it suspiciously before reaching for it.

"Before you unroll that, you should know that I'm relatively certain it's real. I wouldn't hand that over to you without being absolutely certain its authenticity was possible. It was delivered by a falcon. It bears your father's signature—or at least has been signed by someone *claiming* to be your father."

Arryn's eyes widened, and she began quickly to unroll the scroll. The Chieftain reached out, stilling her hand.

"The bird allowed me to see his memories. Aeris sent him to a dark druid down south. He read it, and retrieved a man from deep inside the cave. The bird watched the man write this. Before you read it, you should know I don't believe anything is going to happen to your father—*if* that was him. They need him alive, so please don't rush off and do anything that would put you in danger."

Arryn stood there for some time, thinking about his words as she shook. Her entire body was vibrating. She finally took a deep breath and finished unrolling the small piece of parchment. The moment her eyes landed on the writing, she gasped and nodded, tears coming to her eyes.

"It's real. That's his handwriting. I used to sit on his desk and watch him write for hours."

Arryn,

You have no idea how I've missed you every day. All I've ever wanted was your safety, which is why I write to you now. You must come to me as quickly as you can. I'm in danger here, and I don't know how much longer I'll be around. I have to see you one last time. I have to see that you're okay. I know it'll be hard, but please come to me. I'm in the southernmost part of the Dark Forest.

-- Love always, Dad

Arryn's worry turned to pure hatred and anger as she read the last line, just under her father's, in different handwriting. "*Make it fast, because I've been waiting to end this for ten years.*"

She nearly growled. "How could you possibly believe he's safe there?"

The Chieftain sighed, obviously having predicted her behavior. "He looked healthy, but there's something wrong with his mind. He's young, so I'm assuming it's induced by toxins. The dark druids are far more versed in poisons and hallucinogens than we are. They have kept him alive for ten years, so there's no way they're just going to kill him now."

Arryn laughed sarcastically. "Aeris has been waiting for the day my father could be used against me, and *now* is the perfect time. You know it as well as I do. Only now, it's not just me who will be affected by this. We are *all* at war. This affects everyone."

"Exactly. They're trying to use him to turn us against each other. They know I would choose logic above all else. They know I won't evacuate the Dark Forest to go on a rescue mission without a strategy, and that fact alone would drive a wedge between us."

There was a tug on her hand, and Arryn looked down, her scowl fading as she looked into the eyes of young Corrine. "Remember what you said?" the little girl asked. "You said he taught you to put the lives of others before yourself."

Arryn gave a heavy sigh as her eyes closed, more tears falling.

"Arryn, I know this is hard. You've said before that you were convinced he was there, so I know you've been thinking about this for a while. You've known this whole time that rushing in would be a bad idea. That was what kept you here. They sent this letter to make sure we would come. They wanted to make sure we would abandon our home, because they know we believe family is everything."

Arryn nodded. "Family *is* everything. That's why I have to find a way to save him."

"And we will. But just remember, your family is bigger now than just you and him. It is *all* of us. Think of Celine and young Corrine. Think of Cathillian and Elysia. Of me. You have more than one person in your family. We *will* save him, but please—just trust me. Please let me help you do this right," the Chieftain pleaded.

.   .   .

HER EYES FOCUSED on the Chieftain's, and she saw just how worried about her he was. More than that, she saw his love for her. He was right that it was unfair for her to ask them to run in and save her father. It would put their lives in danger, because it would be a spur-of-the-moment decision.

Still, it didn't make her feel any better about leaving him in a terrible situation. The difference between now and all that time before was that she hadn't been *sure* he was alive, much less that he was truly with the dark druids. Now, she knew without any doubt, and it was eating her alive.

Finally, Arryn nodded. "Fine, but I want to see that falcon. I need to see my father."

As THE DARK druids returned to their familiar territory, Aeris and Jenna fanned out, giving orders for everyone to re-establish camp. The people moved about quickly, not wanting to disappoint their Chieftain, Jerick, or Aeris.

After Jenna had wrapped up her orders to those under her direct command, she located her brother. "Have you checked in with Jace?"

Aeris briefly looked around, making sure no prying eyes or ears were near while pretending to scrutinize his subordinates. "Yes, and so far, everything has gone according to plan. He told me what he wrote in the letter, and that the falcon did as he was asked. Now, we just have to wait and see how effective it will be."

She nodded. "What did the Chieftain say when you told him about the plan? You did say that you were going to, yes?"

"I had to. While we have ulterior motives for all this, we still needed him to give the order to head north in case she didn't take the bait. As far as he knows, we sent the falcon north for the sole purpose of separating Arryn from the herd. If it works, Arryn will come our way soon. If not, we'll need the Chieftain to back me up in going north."

"And he's not concerned with rushing this? He doesn't want to sit and create an elaborate plan to go north?" Jenna asked as she unrolled a bear's hide on the ground. It was what Alexander would do, so it seemed strange Alaric wouldn't want to do it, too.

"He's arrogant. He believes we're invincible now that we have Jerick, but I don't believe that at all. He wanted to kill all of them when we get there, but I convinced him not to. I reminded him just how strong Alexander was when he left, and how much more powerful he has become. I also reminded him of what you said about Arryn, and now he's satisfied with my plan. Separate Arryn from the rest and bring her here."

Jenna looked around, watching their people scurry about as they set camp back up as it had been before they left. "When are we leaving?"

"In a few hours. Just before sunset. I'm going to go help the Chieftains grow the plants we need to make this possible. Everyone needs to wear leather gloves. According to them, if it gets on the skin, they will immediately become very sick, and they may even die." Aeris reached high into the sky and leaned back, stretching his tall body from the tension of a long day.

Jenna nodded, then paused. "I'll make sure everyone's ready. And, Aeris? I *know* Arryn. We won't have to go all the way to the villages. She'll come. I have no doubt about that."

BAST AWOKE to the sound of her sister stirring. They had agreed to stay in Arcadia long enough to make sure the infection wouldn't return. They needed Cleo strong enough to make it to the Dark Forest.

"Hey, could I trouble you for some water?" Cleo asked.

Without answering, Bast climbed out of bed and poured her

another glass. She set the pitcher back down on the nightstand and helped her sister into a sitting position.

"Thank you," Cleo muttered as she took the glass and began sipping from it.

"Are you sure you're strong enough to make the trip?" Bast asked. "You're healing—I can see that—but you're still weak. You can hardly sit up on your own."

Cleo waved a hand as she finished the last bit of water in the cup. "Don't worry about me. I'll be just fine, especially if we can get to those druid people. If they can heal me, everything will have been worth it."

"And what if we meet more bandits on the road? From what Sven has said, he and his brother, Ren, have run into several groups like the one we dealt with. They're quite common at this point. No one knows what they're doing with the crystals, but they assume they're selling them to people with far more money than Arcadia has."

Cleo snorted. "Sounds about right. There's always someone bigger and stronger, or in this case fatter and richer, to take advantage of everyone else. It's probably someone who doesn't have any interest in taking Arcadia, but wants to build their own city."

There was a knock on the door and both girls looked at it, saying, "Come in" in unison.

The door opened, and Amelia stepped inside. "I thought I heard voices. You guys going back to sleep, or are you up for the day?"

Amelia had invited the girls to stay with her, so she could keep an eye on them, make sure they were safe. They had found her to be very kind, so they accepted, not having the ability to pay for anything else.

Cleo shook her head. "Nope. I need to get up and start moving around. I can't lay in this bed anymore. My entire body aches from resting too long."

"Yeah, but rest was what you needed," Bast said.

Cleo rolled her eyes as she sat up farther, then twisted around slowly and placed her feet on the floor. "Yeah, yeah. I heard you the last few days. I'll be fine."

Amelia smiled. "Bast, would you mind coming with me for a moment? Let's give her some space so she can get up without an audience. I get a little pissy when I'm trying to do things for myself when healing, and other people stand around and watch me like I'm some kind of wounded bird. We can make breakfast."

"*Thank* you!" Cleo said, looking at her sister with a sarcastic expression. "At least *someone* around here respects me."

Bast rolled her eyes as she stood and made her way out the door, following Amelia to the kitchen.

I'm going to work in this kitchen and pretend it's all about cooking, but it's not. I need to talk to you, and I don't want Cleo to know because she isn't in any condition to help—though we both know she would try.

Bast looked taken aback for a moment, but then nodded.

Anything I say mentally, respond in your mind. Anything I say out loud, respond out loud. I know her type. If she suspects something, she'll beat it out of us if she must, Amelia sent telepathically.

Bast nodded again.

"There's a skillet in that cabinet down there. Can you grab that for me please?" Amelia asked aloud. *You obviously know about the problems with the bandits. We've been trying to track them and take them down, but it hasn't gone well. Yesterday we received a tip they might attack slightly closer to Arcadia.*

Bast continued to dig in the cabinet before producing a skillet and handing it to Amelia. "Found it. Here you go." She followed that up with, *Does this mean Arcadia's in danger? And are you asking for my help? Is that why you don't want Cleo to know?*

Amelia took the skillet and set it down, gathering the various other items she needed.

"Thank you. Now, if you don't mind, get me the small box of eggs." Amelia lit the flame on the stove before continuing telepathically. *Arcadia is in no danger. These people are stealing supplies to sell to others. And yes, I'm asking for your help. I'll be accompanying a group of guardsmen south on the road. We're using Ren and Sven as bait. We've already sent them south with a small group of Guard following. They've filled the carts with regular stones, covered them, and are bringing them to Arcadia.*

Bast busied herself and did her best to keep up the act.

Ah, so it looks like they're traveling north with new crystals when they cross the path of those assholes, Bast responded telepathically as she handed the eggs to Amelia. "Here you go. Anything else I can do to help?"

"Uh, you can start peeling and slicing potatoes, if you don't mind." Amelia set the box on the counter as she continued to work. *The Guard with them are following at a safe distance, and you and I will head there with another group. Are you in? Because if so, I have belladonna tea ready for your sister.*

Bast smiled as she continued to cut potatoes. They heard footsteps enter the room, and turned to see Cleo give a weak wave and smile before plopping down at the table.

"I think we should leave this morning," Cleo said. "I'm feeling pretty good."

That's code for "I want to get into some trouble," Bast thought to Amelia. "Let's see how you feel after breakfast," she said out loud to her sister

Amelia smiled as she mixed the eggs. *Was that code for "Let's see how you feel after drinking belladonna tea?"*

"Are you kidding? I feel great." Cleo shifted in her seat, her entire face twisting as she fought pain. "Never felt better."

Bast sighed and rolled her eyes again. *Apparently, yes. We're going to have to give her the fucking tea before she kills herself.*

CHAPTER THIRTEEN

After everyone was fed and Cleo had finished her tea, she began to yawn. She couldn't believe just how tired she was, so Amelia and Bast very easily convinced her to lie down for a little while longer.

Amelia had asked Doctor Clarice to sit with Cleo while they were away and monitor her as she slept, so neither one of them felt *entirely* bad for drugging her. After all, they had done it for a good cause.

One, she needed more rest, though she was determined not to get it. And two, they needed to be able to stop the group of bandits without having to worry about Cleo harming herself further.

It took them nearly an hour to reach their destination, but when they did, they weren't disappointed.

I can hear them, Amelia sent to Bast and the five guards traveling with them.

They slowed their horses to a stop, then climbed down. It was still early enough that the sun hadn't yet risen completely over the mountains to the east, which led into the Madlands. They made sure to stick to the shadows and tall grass as they made their way forward.

Everyone get low, Amelia told them. *I can see them up ahead. They're hiding behind that small patch of trees. Sven and Ren should come through any time now.*

They sat patiently, but Bast could feel adrenaline kick in as her excitement grew. That first fight with the bandits had been her first real fight ever. She had been in minor brawls with boys back home who thought girls weren't strong enough to be warriors, but as far as real battles went, the fight alongside Sven was their first.

She was ready for another.

Bast had never truly been able to test her abilities, except in private training sessions or when she and Cleo were alone. In that regard, her journey was becoming more and more exciting all the time.

Amelia and Bast looked at one another as they heard horses' hooves hitting the worn path. The rearick were close.

Bast turned her focus toward the patch of trees Amelia had pointed out earlier, and saw the group of men moving around quite a bit more. She couldn't tell what they were doing in the low light, but it looked as though they were gearing up for something.

How fast can you run? Amelia asked.

Bast turned to her and smiled. *Even if I carried you on my back, I could still outrun anyone here. I might even be as fast as our horses by myself. I'll have to race one sometime.*

Amelia's eyes widened, clearly shocked by the response. Bast had explained that her magic made her stronger and faster than most people, but she hadn't elaborated on just how *much* faster or stronger.

The hoofbeats came within range of the trees ahead, and Bast shifted to a running position, her hands on the ground in front of her and her legs poised to propel her forward.

"Everyone *run*," Amelia hissed in a loud whisper as they saw the bandits fan out from behind the trees.

Bast's eyes flashed blue, and she felt the tingles of power flowing through her body. As soon as she felt them reach her feet she jumped ten feet ahead and broke into a sprint.

Within seconds, she had reached her destination, but she didn't stop. Once again, she leapt forward, propelling herself through the air and tumbling over once before planting both feet in the back of one of the bandits. She used the momentum from the kick to throw her into a backflip again before landing gracefully.

Men ran at her, blades raised as they screamed their war cries. She dropped to her knees, then rolled out of the way as a man swung his sword at her head. After getting back up, she swept the man's legs before chopping him hard in the throat and crushing his larynx.

More circled around her, and she once again pushed her magic through her legs and jumped high enough to clear their heads. As she landed behind one of them she punched him hard in the lower spine, shoving power through her hand into his back. The tiny bones and fragile nerves inside were crushed as he fell to the ground, screaming but unable to move.

She turned just in time to see a man swinging his sword, but before she could react a large fireball hit him in the side. Amelia ran up, her eyes coal black.

Bast was hit hard from the side by a man twice her size punching her hard across her brow bone. She fell to her knees, disoriented for a moment. He grabbed her braid, wrapping it around his hand as he yanked back.

"You stupid bitch. You're *really* not gonna like what happens next," he said.

She groaned as he pulled harder, but then she smiled. "If that means what I think it does, *you're* not gonna like it either."

She thrust an elbow back, hitting him hard in the balls. He

cried out and his grip on her hair loosened immediately. She spun around on her knees and knocked his hands away from his groin, gripping his manhood in her hand and squeezing.

"Clearly, your daddy never taught you how to treat a lady. And considering I'm a sixteen-year-old girl, that makes you an even bigger piece of shit. You won't be needing this anymore," she said before crushing it in her hand and pulling as hard as she could. She could feel the flesh tear as the endowment was freed from his body.

She stood and kicked him over, leaving him screaming as she wiped the blood from her hand on her pants and surveyed the area.

***

Though Bast had told Amelia how fast she could move and how hard she could hit, there was still a big part of her that hadn't quite believed it. She had thought Bast was exaggerating, but when Amelia had told everyone to run, she was proven wrong.

Bast had all but exploded into a sprint that was far faster than anything she had ever seen. Amelia and the others ran as hard as they could, but it took a lot longer to reach the bandits than she would have liked.

As she and her men hurried toward the fight, Sven, Ren, their men, and the guards she had sent to trail them met the bandits head-on. Bast also arrived and established herself immediately as a large threat, but there were so many bandits that Amelia worried Bast might be overcome soon, even with her impressive strength.

Amelia and her guards arrived just in time. A sword was about to come down on Bast, but Amelia was faster. Her eyes flashed black, her arms arcing over her chest before she threw a large fireball which struck Bast's attacker directly in the ribs.

Once he was down, she threw another at a man attacking Sven.

Amelia had spent weeks in the Dark Forest training with Elysia and Nika while Arryn was missing, and with the mystics during the long wait for the battle against Scarlett for Arcadia. She was more skilled with a sword than any of the outlaws she was about to engage in battle.

A tall, chubby man ran up on her right with a sword in his hand. She dodged his first swing and ducked under the second when he opted for speed instead of precision. He slashed and slashed again. "Keep slicing until I hit something" seemed to be his style of fighting.

She dodged again, this time kicking out as hard as she could. The toe of her boot connected with his ribs, and he cried out, his grip on the sword loosening. She stepped forward and stomped on his foot before driving her fist hard across his face. He wavered a bit, and she grabbed his sword and ran it straight through his chest.

After pulling the blade free, she spun and lifted it, the clang of metal on metal ringing in her ears as her sword stopped another. The man grimaced and pushed harder, and Amelia's entire body locked up as she tried to keep his sword from coming down on her.

She growled and grunted as she pushed back—hard enough this time to force him back a couple steps. She looked at him and said, "Fuck this."

Her eyes flashed black again as she flexed her entire body, jerking it forward as her hands shot out. An invisible force shoved the man, and he stared at her as he stumbled backward several feet.

She smiled and dropped the sword, then slowly lifted her hands from her sides. The ground began to shake a little under their feet as she felt for rocks in the earth.

He turned and began to run, but she was faster. She jerked her hands upward, and small stones burst from the ground. When she twisted her hand, several shot directly toward him, one driving straight through the back of his skull and dropping him.

Her arsenal of various size rocks went with her as she stepped farther onto the battlefield. Bast was fighting two men, but the young woman made quick work of each. She crushed the skull of one with her fist before kicking the other several feet back, the man flying through the air before hitting the ground hard.

Amelia heard footsteps all around her, and she swiped her hands to split the rocks apart, impaling the three men running at her. They dropped dead, and she allowed her eyes to fade back to normal.

If she used much more heavy magic, she wouldn't have the energy to finish the fight.

And given how many she and Bast had taken out already, it *was* almost finished. But she wanted to bring at least one of them back with her for questioning. She needed to know why these attacks were happening.

SVEN FOUGHT hard next to his brother, each swinging his war hammer. They had been in many fights with remnant over the years, and they had been together for a lot of those, but Sven was happy to be fighting alongside his little brother this time.

They were sick of people taking advantage of them and their people. They'd had enough of those piece-of-shit stragglers stealing what they had worked hard for. Unlike battles with the remnant, this fight was personal, and having his brother along for the ride made it somehow even more satisfying.

A man came at Ren from behind, and Sven struck him hard in the leg with his hammer, crushing the bandit's hip and femur in the process. Ren turned and finished him off with a hit directly to the man's head.

Ren had worried about the girl, but that quickly faded as he watched her drop twice as many men as he and his brother combined.

The fight was beginning to wind down, as the two rearick fought together. The Arcadian Guard hadn't been very useful, but at least they had kept the bastards busy enough for Sven and Ren to take them down.

Sven ducked and rammed his war hammer into the soft belly of one of the bandits before pulling back and swinging hard at the man's chest, easily taking him out. Just as he was about to turn for another, Ren took the new attacker out instead.

They both heaved for breath. Neither had done much fighting in years up until recently, and each of them were getting older. It was getting harder on them, but they still had it.

"How many're yers, Brother?" Sven asked.

Ren looked at the bodies on the ground. "I dunno, but I'm bettin' at least twice whatever ye had. Just count up however many're yers, 'n double it. That's mine."

Sven laughed, the effort causing him to cough a few times before he finished. "I bet."

"Is everyone all right?" Amelia asked as she ran up.

The rearick brothers looked at one another and shrugged before turning back to Amelia and nodding. "Good enough," they said together, and chuckled.

It appeared everyone had survived, and no one was severely injured. Even Amelia seemed impressed by that.

"I thought I'd lose at least a few Guard, or they'd be injured for sure. I guess I have the two of you to thank for preventing that," Amelia said to the rearick.

"Amelia," Bast said.

Amelia turned toward the voice. "Yes? Is everything okay? Are you all right?"

Bast nodded. "I left one alive. Not purposely, mind you. I

punched him in the spine and it paralyzed him. I thought he would die, but it was low enough that he survived."

Amelia sighed in relief. "Good. By the time I realized I wanted to take one alive, we'd killed almost everyone. Now I might be able to figure out what the hell is going on around here."

Amelia gave orders to her guards to clear out a cart for him, since she didn't want him injured further in case it killed him.

"Now, let's hurry up and get back to my house before your sister wakes up and kills us both," Amelia said.

Bast only laughed, knowing it was true.

CHAPTER FOURTEEN

Alaric and Jerick led the way north with the large group behind them, ready for whatever might happen. The plan was simple—Aeris had seen to that. He was impressed by the younger man's ambition to separate the girl from the rest of her team. If what he had heard about her was true, he definitely didn't want her on Alexander's side.

If he could somehow manage to force her to switch sides using her father as leverage, it was possible the odds of his winning the war for the Dark Forest would tip in his favor—not that he'd had many doubts once his brother had joined him.

It was now nightfall, and they were approaching the southern part of the barrier. As long as they stayed far enough away that any wandering patrol on the other side couldn't hear or sense them, they would be able to carry out their plan without issue.

Alaric raised a hand, signaling everyone in the group to stop. He then waved the small group who were carrying the poisonous leaves forward. They spent the entire day before they left growing the deadly plant, giving them bags and bags full of it.

Along the way others had gathered sticks and kindling that would allow the plants to burn slower and create big smoke clouds. The plant itself burned slowly because of the poisonous oil it naturally contained, and according to Jerick, would create large plumes of smoke on its own. The rest would just help it along.

Within twenty minutes, his group was ready, and he hoped Aeris and Jenna were in place along the eastern wall as well. Though Alaric couldn't call wind as easily as he once had without exhausting himself, his brother could.

At another silent gesture, several dark druids began lighting the leaves, sticks, and small branches that had been divided among the twenty people in charge of starting the assault.

Jerick signaled for everyone to get back, and they quickly retreated several yards. Even Alaric took several steps back, not wanting to be in his brother's way.

After the first few fires were successfully lit, the dark druids who had started them began to cough and stumbled backward out of the way. Jerick's eyes flashed a dim green, his arms lifting from his sides as a light breeze began to blow toward the barrier.

It wasn't enough to inhibit the others from starting their fires, but it was enough to keep the smoke blowing toward and through the barrier.

The dark druids lit their fires all the way to the end, and jumped out of the way as quickly as possible once they caught. When Jerick strengthened his magical wind, large plumes of smoke billowed through the barrier.

Alaric heard a loud thump to his left and quickly turned.

The dark druid who had been felled by the smoke was seizing on the ground, foaming at the mouth and choking.

"I thought you said we would be able to process this through our bodies since we're used to toxins," Alaric said to his brother.

Jerick laughed. "I said I *believed* that would be so, and I still do. Look—that idiot didn't wear the gloves Aeris instructed everyone to wear. He also took a direct hit from the smoke, undiluted by the oxygen around it. Relax. That's what he gets for disobeying."

His brother was certainly right about that. Alaric couldn't stand it when they ignored him. His concern wasn't the loss of life, but that there was loss of life when there *shouldn't* have been. If that idiot could die, then so could he… but his brother's explanation satisfied him.

He smiled as he watched the smoke wafting through the Dark Forest barrier like a thick, heavy fog. It wouldn't be long, and he would have exactly what he needed. He would have the warrior that would win him the war.

If it hadn't been for Aeris, he would've attempted for a hell of a lot more. He would have made his way through that barrier and taken the lives of everyone who stood in his way. He would cut down any in his path until he found his true target. His destiny.

Alexander.

Unfortunately for him, Aeris had made several good points, the best of those being that Alexander was not the same man he had dealt with years ago. He was much stronger, and he might even be able to withstand the effects of the smoke.

This truly was the safest way to go, and a little patience would go a long way to securing his success. Taking Arryn would damage them emotionally and potentially leave them powerless against him.

Arryn sighed heavily and quietly stepped outside. It was late, and everyone was already in bed asleep or out patrolling. She had made sure to stay close to Elysia that day, so she knew exactly where the warriors would be at various times during the night.

She had calculated a route to get out of the Dark Forest and move south. She planned to take Snow with her, but once she got close enough to the dark druid camp, Snow would have to stay behind. She would need to be subtle, and a large white tiger was certainly not the way to do it.

Without saying a word, Arryn reached through the bond and called Snow. As the Chieftain had requested, she had taken more than a day to think things over. He had told her that if she could come up with a plan that wouldn't leave the Dark Forest weak, he would help her.

Though she had tried, she hadn't been able to think of anything that didn't risk the people she loved. In the end, this had been the only plan that made sense to her, but she couldn't tell the Chieftain. If she had, he would've done all he could to stop her.

She had found that falcon and had seen the images he carried. Aeris and the others traveling back to the southernmost part of the Forest. Her father and the weakened state he appeared to be in. Most importantly, she had heard the things that dark druid had said to him.

Though the falcon might not have understood entirely what those words meant, when she heard them through his memory, she had picked out enough to understand.

Her father was in real danger. He was paranoid that Adrien was coming for him, as well as for her. He had no idea that Adrien was dead, and he didn't realize she had grown up. Whatever they had done to him, they had been doing it since she was a child. He had no idea how much time had passed.

And that posed problems of its own.

If she got there and tried to save him, but he had no idea who she was, it would put her in danger as well as him. She needed him to believe without hesitation or emotion.

She hoped she could heal him enough to recognize her. According to the Chieftain, his demented state had probably been caused by poisons and hallucinogenic plants like mushrooms. It would take time because of the many years they had been dosing him, but he could be healed of the damage.

And she wouldn't stop until he was himself again.

She and Snow pelted through the Dark Forest, the wind

picking up as they ran. Arryn felt a tickle in her throat and reached for the canteen she carried on her hip. At first, the water helped, but then the irritation became worse.

She saw fog rolling in, but she realized the amount of moisture in the air wasn't right for it. She began to cough, and even Snow seemed to sense something was off and slowed down.

Snow sent up an alarm as she came to an abrupt stop, then turned and ran back toward the village. No words were needed as Arryn reached through the bond to see what had frightened her so.

Her eyes widened as she looked back over her shoulder. The mist that was quickly approaching was not truly fog.

"Snow, stop now!" Arryn ordered. The big cat stopped quickly, and Arryn jumped off and turned toward the smoke. "*Run*. Run as fast as you can and wake the Chieftain, wake Cathillian, wake Elysia, wake everyone. Start with the Elders."

She covered her mouth as she began coughing again, pulling her hand back with blood spattered across her palm. "The smoke is poison. It's what Corrine warned us about. Go, Snow. Save as many as you can!"

The tiger briefly butted her head against Arryn's shoulder, silently telling her that she loved her before she did as her master had asked.

Arryn turned back toward the smoke, her eyes flashing green as she lifted her arms out to her sides. She fought the urge to take a deep breath, knowing it would only do more damage. As she called her magic, hoping to bring enough wind to blow the smoke back, she was hit with another coughing fit.

Since lives were in danger, she pushed as hard as she could, but only a light breeze blew out around her. At that moment, she felt her entire body shake, and her eyes grew heavy. Fear began to crush her as darkness closed on her.

"Bitch help you all when I wake up," she said just before her eyes rolled back, and she collapsed to the ground.

CHAPTER FIFTEEN

Zoe awoke with a start, lifting her hand to wipe the thin layer of sweat from her forehead. She'd had a terrible dream regarding a letter she had received earlier in the day.

One of the mystics of the temple had sent it to her to let her know that Julianne was on her way back, and also that the bandit problem with the rearick on the road to Arcadia had gotten worse.

She had meant to talk with Arryn about it, to ask her opinion, but she had never gotten a chance. As she sat there shaking on the edge of her bed, she regretted that.

She dreamt she had been attacked by a group of bandits on her way home. During the fight, she somehow managed to save herself while watching everyone else in her party die horrible deaths.

Fearing another dream like that, she stepped out of the guest-house and made her way to Arryn's house.

She knocked on the door, but no one answered. That wasn't completely strange, since the girl usually slept like a rock, but when she reached out with her mind she felt nothing. Zoe rushed through the door, but Arryn was gone.

Zoe thought back through the day and remembered that Arryn wasn't part of the night patrol. She very rarely took that assignment because of her heavy training responsibilities—even Zoe had learned that in her short time here. She then remembered how Arryn had clung to Elysia that day as orders were given for the night shift.

At that time Arryn was generally in her seat by the fire.

"Shit!" Zoe ran out the door.

She rushed to the Chieftain's hut, knocking as hard as she could, knowing he'd had quite a bit to drink that night. The druids apparently had to drink far more than the average human to get any effect because of their bodies' natural ability to heal and filter toxins.

When she didn't get an answer, she ran next door to Elysia's house. She didn't even have the chance to knock before the door was flung open and the worried Elder stepped outside.

"Zoe? What is it?" Elysia asked, her face and voice strong.

Zoe shook her head. "I could be wrong, but I think Arryn's gone. She's not in her house, and I know you didn't put her on duty tonight. Snow's nowhere around either."

The Chieftain wandered up, yawning, but quickly regained his authoritative posture. "You think she's gone?"

"Who's gone?" Corrine asked, walking outside the hut that stood on the opposite side of Arryn's. She was clutching her blanket tight to her chest. "Is it Arryn?"

Zoe sighed as she looked to the small girl, Elysia and the Chieftain doing the same.

"Go back to bed, sweetheart," Elysia said, obviously struggling to keep her voice calm while still holding an edge to let her know she meant it. "Everything's fine."

Corrine shook her head. "No, it isn't. I heard Zoe knocking on Arryn's door and say 'shit.' Arryn went after her dad, didn't she?"

The Chieftain reached for Zoe's arm, turning her attention back to him. "Are you sure that's what happened?"

Zoe nodded. "I pay attention to people. It's just part of who I am, and being a mystic. I notice patterns, and I've learned that people rarely deviate from their usual behavior. Still, something didn't click tonight. Arryn was following Elysia around instead of sitting by the fire with her usual bowl of fruit or mug of weak, sweet wine."

Elysia's eyes closed as she sighed, her head falling back. "She needed to know where the warriors were gonna be, so she could leave without anyone knowing. *Dammit.*"

"It's possible she hasn't been gone long," the Chieftain said. "Let's fan out and see if we can find her."

"I'm going, too!" Corrine said, throwing the blanket she had been holding down to the ground.

The Chieftain grabbed her shoulders to still her. "No, you need to go back inside and get to sleep. We'll find her. Everything will be okay."

She yanked herself away from his grasp, her expression angry. "No! Arryn's everything to me. I've survived on my own all this time. I think I'm more than capable of looking for someone."

Sighing, the Chieftain nodded. "Fine. You're with me, kid. You know… You take after her more and more all the time."

Corrine and the Chieftain began to run south as Elysia and Zoe stopped to beat on Cathillian's door, waking him for the search party. Within moments he was up and out the door, ready to help the moment his mother said the words, "Arryn is missing, and we need to find her."

Zoe only hoped the young woman had left for a walk to think things over, but deep down she knew that wasn't the case.

As Corrine and the Chieftain moved south, they noticed fog moving in from the east.

"Do you smell that?" Corrine asked as they ran. As soon as she asked, she broke into a coughing fit, falling to the ground and wheezing.

"Corrine!" the Chieftain shouted as he dropped to her side, his eyes flashing green as he pushed power through her.

A loud roar sounded out, and the Chieftain sensed Snow's rapid approach, but Arryn wasn't with her. Suddenly, he grew weaker and began to cough as breathing became harder and harder. Within seconds, blackness surrounded him, and he collapsed to the ground next to Corrine.

Snow ran as fast as she could back to the southern village. The smoke had gotten much worse, but she stayed underneath most of it —and it didn't seem to have the same effect on her as it did on Arryn.

She came across Zoe and the Chieftain lying on the ground. Knowing she would be unable to carry both, Snow did the only thing she could. She lowered herself to the ground and took a deep breath before roaring as loudly as she could.

In seconds, Zobig's roar came back. The colossal animals didn't get along very well, but they understood a cry for help and what it might mean.

Snow rolled Corrine onto her stomach before grabbing the back of her clothes, then lifted her and began to run. Within moments, Snow heard the heavy footfalls of the large black bear coming toward them. When they met, each regarded the other with respect, and Snow sent him after the Chieftain.

The white tiger bypassed the village entirely and ran straight to the river before dropping the girl by the bank, then headed back to wake Elysia and the others.

When she got there, people were already scurrying about. She realized Elysia, Cathillian, and Zoe were looking for Arryn. The group, having heard Snow's roar earlier and more than likely

Zobig's answer as well, believed something was wrong with Arryn.

Snow ran in and slid to a stop, growling as she began tugging on Elysia's arm. Elysia quickly reached out with her free hand and laid it on the side of the big cat's face as her eyes flashed green.

The tiger could feel the brush of the Elder's power as she communicated to Elysia what had happened. She showed Elysia the images of Arryn telling her to find everyone and get them out.

Elysia also saw the girl coughing up blood.

Elysia's green eyes widened as she turned to Cathillian. "Wake everyone and get them to the river quickly! The dark druids are blowing poisonous smoke into the village. Arryn is trying to use wind to blow it back out, but the Chieftain and Corrine are down. Snow sent Zobig after the Chieftain, and Corrine's already on the riverbank. *Hurry!*"

A worried Zoe stepped forward as Cathillian ran off, obvious fear on her face. "If people are already down, how will we evacuate them?"

Elysia reached for the girl's hand. "We will have to start ripping people out of their beds and using vines to move them through the trees. This is going to take an enormous amount of magic, but we can do it. I need you, too. Go around the village and send out warnings with your magic. Wake everyone you can and implant a sense of urgency to run toward the river."

Zoe nodded. "I can definitely do that."

Elysia turned to Snow. "You've done an amazing job. Now go bust into houses and drag people out of bed if you have to. Get them to the river."

Snow took a deep breath and let loose with another very long, painfully loud roar, nearly causing Elysia to cover her ears. Almost immediately, Elysia heard the howls of the wolves in the village, many of which were familiars, and the loud hoofbeats of the familiar horses, Chaos being one of those.

Echo called out from overhead, and Elysia realized at that moment that Snow had alerted every one of them.

The large animals followed as Snow took off running. She could hear the tiger grumbling as she reached the first house, slamming her front paws against the door and throwing it wide open before growling loudly just inside.

Once the animals saw her do this, they began to spread out, busting the doors in and running inside before howling, and in some cases, dragging people out.

For a moment, Elysia was overwhelmed by the actions of their familiars. They were working as a team to save everyone, not just their individual druid.

Elysia ran for Chaos, jumping onto his back and riding for Nika's house. When she arrived, Nika was already dressed and stumbling out the door.

"What the hell's going on?" Nika asked.

"The dark druids have attacked using deadly smoke, the very thing Corrine told us about. Familiars are waking people, but I saw a few dragging some. I don't know if they were alive or dead. We have to get everyone out."

"Luna!" Nika shouted as she climbed on Chaos' back with Elysia.

"Snow called all the familiars, so Luna is probably with her."

"Seriously? Did you know they could do that?" Nika asked.

Elysia shook her head as Chaos began to run for the village again. "I'm not surprised by anything anymore. I've seen them do it on a small scale, but I didn't realize Snow had established herself as the dominant. I've never seen anything like that."

"We have to find Dante," Nika said.

Elysia didn't respond as they reached the village. Everything was chaotic, and people were running everywhere. Smoke had begun to fill the area, and Elysia almost immediately felt the effects.

"I'll call wind," Elysia said. "You go find Dante."

Elysia's eyes flashed green as she dismounted and walked farther into the village. Facing southeast, she surrounded herself with power and a gentle breeze began to blow, then blew even harder.

She began to cough and felt weakness in her knees, but she couldn't let up. The village needed to be evacuated quickly. People were being carried out, and some of them weren't moving.

A hand rested on her shoulder, and she almost immediately began to feel better. Looking behind her, she saw Cathillian's green eyes glowing as he pushed his magic through her.

Even though her own magic continued to flow out of her, she felt much stronger because of the healing. Now that the smoke was out of the immediate area around her, she was able to breathe clearly, and Cathillian stepped away.

Beside his mother, Cathillian raised his hands and added his power to hers. "We have no idea how long this will last, so I figured you could use some help."

She nodded. "That's true, and I did. Thank you. Don't use large gusts—just a heavy breeze. Only strong enough to keep the smoke from blowing this direction. As long as we keep it simple, we should be able to maintain it for a while."

Cathillian nodded, opting for silence as each of them focused on what was around them.

"I found Dante," Nika said as she ran up. "He's hiding high in a tree, and for once that was a good thing. I told him to stay put. I also ran into Ryel. We're mobilizing all the warriors and taking to the trees to travel over the smoke. We're going to fan out and make sure the dark druids aren't inside."

Cathillian snorted. "If *we* can't handle this, as strong as we are, how the hell could they?"

"Their bodies are used to breaking down hazardous substances. It's possible they can walk straight through this and not be affected," Elysia said. "We definitely need to check the area. Nika, go ahead, but please be careful. If any of you feel the slightest tingle in the back of your throat, get your asses back. Search for any fallen warriors on patrol as well. We had several along the southern and eastern borders."

Nika saluted Elysia before her eyes flashed and a vine pulled her high into the tree.

THE CHIEFTAIN COUGHED and coughed again, rolling to his side just in time to throw up. He hadn't done that in many, many years—and he didn't like it.

He struggled to sit up, his eyes blurry. He remembered the smoke, but the grass around him didn't feel the same as it had when he fell.

He was somewhere new.

He tried to focus his eyes, but his head was splitting. It felt as though there were a vice squeezing his chest relentlessly. There was a loud rattle and wheeze every time he took a breath, but it was slowly getting better.

Still unable to see, he did what he could to focus his power to heal himself, but it was useless. Nothing would come.

Just then, a hand touched the side of his face. It was warm and soft, and it grew even warmer as power radiated through him. His next breath cleared as he took it in.

Slowly, his vision came back, and his head quit pounding. He was looking into the face of Clara, a mute druid warrior with a unique magical gift that allowed her to communicate tele-pathically.

Relax. You're safe now. There are too many to heal completely, but I made an exception for you, she sent to the Chieftain.

He smiled and nodded. "Thank you. What has happened?"

The village has been evacuated, and almost everyone is here. I helped get people free and then stayed to heal those who were badly injured by the smoke. Some were just dizzy, but others had passed out. Unfortunately, some were lost.

Rage filled the Chieftain. How easily the dark druids had attacked, using a single poisonous plant. He could never even *imagine* fighting so cruelly, but even if he had, it wouldn't have had the same effect on them.

And that was a weakness.

"Has anyone seen Arryn? She went missing before all this happened. And young Corrine. How is she? Is she all right?"

Clara nodded, grabbing his hand to comfort him. *The young one is just fine. She's awake now and sitting by the edge of the river, healing and resting. As far as Arryn goes, I haven't seen her, and I don't think anyone else has either. But I do know that if it hadn't been for Arryn, we would all be dead.*

"What you mean?"

Arryn sent Snow after us. Elysia spoke to Snow, so she saw the images. Arryn stayed in the middle of all that smoke and sent Snow back to warn us. She was going to try to blow the smoke out.

Dread filled the Chieftain as he looked toward the village. "But all of us are here, and many were damaged in some way by the smoke. If it reached the village, she was unsuccessful. That means she must've fallen."

Clara swallowed hard as her hand gently covered her mouth. *I hadn't thought of that. Oh, my God. We have to clear the smoke and look for her.*

Another warrior ran into the area, searching until he locked eyes with Clara. Running over, he saluted both her and the Chieftain. "The smoke is regressing. Elysia and Cathillian have been blowing it out of the village, but it seems to be dissipating on its own as well."

"Has anyone seen a dark druid?" the Chieftain asked.

The warrior shook his head. "No, not one."

Clara looked confused. *Why would they launch such a successful attack but not come into the Forest? I have to say, this was the best plan they've ever had, and it was working flawlessly. Why would they just leave?*

Realization struck the Chieftain. He sighed and shook his head, his nostrils flaring in anger as his eyes closed and his fists clenched. "They would only leave if they had what they wanted."

"What did they come for?" the warrior asked.

Clara gasped as she looked at the Chieftain in both shock and horror.

The Chieftain loosened his fists before tightening them again. "Arryn."

CHAPTER SIXTEEN

Walking through the Forest was always bumpy, but alternating between being carried over someone's shoulder and being dragged on a makeshift stretcher was far worse.

As Arryn was moved through the Dark Forest, she slipped in and out of consciousness, mostly when she was being jostled the worst. At that point, she preferred her abduction by Talia and Scarlett—they had been gentler, even with slitting her wrists along the way.

Several times along the way, she was awake, but unable to move or speak. That was slowly starting to change.

She could feel the pounding in her head, the throbbing ache threatening to split it in two. Then she began coughing again, unable to stop. She threw up all over herself once because she was unable to roll over, and one of her captors hit her for it, which knocked her out again.

She had no idea how long she was unconscious that time, but when she awoke, that splitting headache was far worse. Her entire body hurt—she imagined that was from the poison as well as the rough way she had been handled.

"Good morning, Sunshine," an unfamiliar voice said to her.

It was still very dark outside, so she knew she had either been out a full day and into the next night or less than a few hours. "This sun sure as shit isn't shining here, Lord of Darkness."

Though she didn't know exactly who he was, and she couldn't see because her vision was still affected by the smoke, she could feel the coldness inside him. He was a black pit of hatred. It could have been any of them, but she had a feeling it was Alaric. Her second guess would have been Aeris, but she knew his voice.

She would never forget it.

The man laughed, and the sound wrapped around her like an icy blanket that had been left outside in winter. Chills raced all throughout her body, further alerting her to the danger she was in.

"You're a funny one," he said.

She smiled, though everything around her was still blurry. "You know, I hear that a lot."

"I believe it. I also believe it gets you in trouble, doesn't it?"

She snorted. "You have no idea. So, Sir Darkness, why don't you do a girl a favor and give her the name of her captor?"

"Judging by the fact you're not looking at me, I'm assuming you can't see. If you could, you'd know that your little nickname suits me. My name is Alaric, but I'm assuming you've heard that name before."

She narrowed her eyes, her lips parting just a bit as she pretended to think. "Alaric. Isn't that usually accompanied by 'dick' or 'jackass?'"

There was a pregnant pause, and she found herself wondering if she was about to get hit again. Finally, he said, "I suppose it is, where you're from."

Brushing off her momentary fear, she smiled and nodded, and pointed a finger even though she had no idea where she was pointing. "Then yes! I *have* indeed heard of you. Say, does anyone around here have anything without any *surprises* in it to drink? I don't fancy the taste of mildew, and poison doesn't sit well with me either. It's embarrassing and all, but..." she leaned forward a bit though it hurt, lifting her hand to the side of her mouth as if to share a secret, "stomach problems. Those pesky poisons go straight through me, if ya know what I mean. Plain water will be just fine." She winked.

She heard a stifled laugh across from her, and she sat back. Well, at least he found her amusing.

"Thirsty, are you? Or are you just trying to get under my skin?"

She sighed. "Funny story. I was walking through the woods with my white tiger and a bunch of fog rolled in, but it wasn't fog at all. It was actually a poisonous cloud of smoke." She snorted, faking an amused laugh. "Some *asshole* pumped a noxious cloud of... Well, I don't know what it was, but it left my throat a little *dry*." She quietly croaked out that last bit with a disgusted expression, touching her fingers to her throat to exaggerate her discomfort.

And though she was messing with him as hard as she could, she really did hope he might give her some water. Her throat really did hurt, but she wasn't going to play nice. She would suffer before she did that.

"I'll have someone bring you some water, and it won't be tainted with anything you don't know about. I trust that you will be on your best behavior here, because if you're not, your father will suffer for it."

Her eyes narrowed again, and she was serious this time. "Won't be tainted with anything I don't know about? What exactly is *that* supposed to mean?"

"Like I just said, I won't add anything you don't know about because I trust you'll be on your best behavior. Even so, I can't exactly let you run around at full strength, now can I? That would be stupid on my part, and despite what you may have heard, 'stupid' is *not* a category I fall into. You will be given a tea that will not make you sick, but it *will* weaken you."

Arryn opened her mouth to speak, but he was quick to interrupt her.

"And you're going to drink it without a fight, because if you don't your father will suffer the consequences. I rather enjoy your sense of humor. In fact, I rather enjoy *you*. You amuse me. I didn't think I would like you, but I do. Let's keep it that way, shall we? No harm will come to you while you're here, and if anyone does harm you, be sure and let me know."

Arryn was beginning to perceive shapes, and she could see him sitting across from her in the moonlight. "What will you do, spank them?"

He laughed. "Arryn, you and I are going to be *great* friends. If anyone dares harm you, I'll kill them. I will kill them to show you exactly how serious I am about our friendship. You are *very* important."

When she swallowed, her throat felt like there was sand grinding against the membranes. "Why am I so important to you? What do you think you'll get out of a friendship with me? And exactly what type of friendship are we talking about here, because I have some boundaries about just how far my friendships go."

She heard another light laugh and saw the shadows in front of her moving, so she assumed he was shaking his head. "Nothing like that, I assure you. But you *are* important. You are the key to me winning this war. You're going to help me fight Alexander. You're going to claim the Dark Forest for me."

She looked at him incredulously. "And why in the hell would I do that? Even if I *had* problems with Alexander—which I don't, and never have—you just tried to kill me, and you tried to kill a lot of other *innocent* people."

His features were finally coming into focus, and she blinked several times. She took a deep breath, hoping it didn't show, when she saw his burnt-charcoal-colored hair, his dark-gray skin, and his ghostly light-gray eyes.

"You'll do it because I have your father. If you don't..." He paused, smiling. "I'm betting you think I'll say that I'm going to kill him. But you should know, Arryn, my *dear* friend, that it's so much worse than that. I will take him apart slowly, piece by piece. I will make you watch as I dismantle him inch by inch. Do you know how long it takes a man to die at that rate?"

Her eyes narrowed as she stared him down, and her rage built. The gentle sound of thunder lightly rolled, and the wind started to blow a bit. His eyes widened as he sat there, a smile spreading across his face as he watched green slowly bleed into her dark-brown irises.

"You should know that threatening me is *never* a good idea. You should also know that when I get out of here, I'm going to open the pits of hell myself and send you there like Alexander should have years ago. Mark my words, because I don't make promises I can't keep."

His smile widened as her eyes grew greener and greener and clouds slowly began to move into the area. "Looks like it's time for that tea, yes? They were right about you, you know. You truly are everything they said. There's no way in hell you should have recovered that quickly, but you did."

He stood, laughing again. "Arryn, remember what I said. We're going to be great friends. The sooner you realize this, the sooner I can let you and your father go once the Dark Forest is mine. And you have my word, I *will* let him go in one piece as long as you help me."

Alaric waved someone over, and they brought a steaming mug. She eyed the man with disgust, trying her hardest to call active magic, but she couldn't. It was right there, but she couldn't touch it.

"Now, now, don't be a bad girl. Drink some tea, get some sleep, and we'll have a family reunion first thing in the morning."

Arryn knew her only choice was to bide her time. If she made any wrong moves while she was weak, her father would be harmed in unimaginable ways.

Unable to see straight anymore because of her intense rage, Arryn lifted her shaky hands and accepted the cup. She took several drinks and handed it back.

"Good girl," Alaric said, before turning to walk away. "Get some rest. I'll see you in the morning."

THE SUN HAD FINALLY BEGUN to rise on the Dark Forest, and nearly everyone who could be healed had been. Echo had flown north to the unaffected villages to recruit healers. By the time they reached the southernmost village twenty were dead, and many more were injured or close to death.

The Chieftain and Elysia made their way through the groups that had elected to stay by the river until their homes could be fully cleaned. They checked on everyone, and assured them things would be fine.

The plan was to take all bedding and anything else water-sensitive out of the homes before removing the leaves that acted as roofs. Once that was done, rain would be called, and the homes would be flooded, washing away any toxins still clinging to the wood or other items inside.

Once that was done, they would be aired and left to dry before the leaves were grown back, once again forming the thick protective roof.

When Elysia and the Chieftain went back to the village, a pissed-off Cathillian awaited them. "Arryn is nowhere to be found. No trace of her anywhere. We have groups of warriors out looking for her, but we've come up with nothing."

The Chieftain was unsure what to do. He had never thought this possible. He had made a mistake by not giving into Arryn.

They had wanted only her all along. If he had gone he might have spared his people this act of war, and it would have made Arryn happy.

He should have helped her go after her father right away, but he had believed in his heart that he was doing the right thing.

To go after Christopher without knowing exactly what they were up against would have risked the lives of many of their warriors. And if they had lost too many, there would have been nothing stopping the dark druids from taking the Dark Forest.

It was possible they had her now. It was possible she was dead or would be soon, or worse. He had to get her back before they hurt her. He needed to get Christopher back as well, as he should have done in the first place.

But what could he do at *this* moment? Everyone was exhausted and weak. Over half the village had been affected horribly, and a good portion of those who hadn't been affected had at least in *some* way weakened themselves healing everyone else.

They were in a worse situation now than they had been before the attack, which only added to his regret.

"What are we going to do? They have her, and I damn well know it. This can't stand, Grandfather. I lost her once, and I'm *not* fucking doing it again," Cathillian ranted, his nostrils flaring, and his fists clenched at his sides.

Elysia turned to her father. "He's right. We can't just let them take her. I know we have the entire tribe to think of, but if it weren't for Arryn, a good number of us, including you and Zoe, would've been dead. And yes, I'm well aware she was more than likely trying to get out of the Dark Forest, given her earlier actions. That doesn't change the fact that she stopped and sent Snow back to save the rest of us. She sacrificed herself for us, and we can't repay that by letting her suffer whatever fate they have planned."

The Chieftain sighed, a long uncomfortable pause falling as

he debated their words. Once again, he was worried about his people as a whole, in comparison to a single life. Logic told him he needed to protect the many, not the one.

But his guiding rule—family above all else—told him he needed to get his ass south.

Cathillian's expression turned even angrier, and the Chieftain held up his hand. "If we attack right now, we *will* fail. It doesn't matter if we take the entire druid army with us, we *will* die. We are all too weak. They plan to use her against us. They're not going to kill her, or they would've left her dead body in the Forest for us to find. We'll take the next few hours to rest. After that, we move south. There's no way in hell I'll let them get away with it."

Though Cathillian still seemed pissed off, he clenched his jaw and nodded, accepting what his grandfather had told him. "Four hours—that's it. We've all learned how to meditate from Zoe, so we can gather more strength on the journey there. No excuses."

He turned and walked away, leaving Elysia and the Chieftain standing there in silence.

But on the sidelines was someone quiet, someone subtle, someone who was used to being unseen. Corrine moved backward, gauging each step carefully so she didn't make a sound. She had heard every word, and knew Arryn was in danger.

Arryn had taught her a great many things, but the best were faith and love. She had taught her those things *did* exist, and good people existed, too. She had taught her family was worth living and dying for.

Arryn had also taught her that putting family above your own wellbeing was what you did when you truly loved someone.

As a vine unrolled from a tree above her, wrapping around her extended arm and down around her waist, Corrine said, "*They* won't go right this minute, but I will."

CHAPTER SEVENTEEN

Waking up was a little too familiar for Arryn. Everything under her felt rocky, and her neck was bent in an uncomfortable position.

She was in a cave.

She sighed as she struggled to sit. Her face was toward the wall, so she rolled onto her back and did her best to push herself upward. Her head still ached, but it wasn't nearly as bad as before —just a dull thrum of pain.

It took a couple minutes, but she was finally able to sit with her back against the cave wall. She pulled her knees to her chest and wrapped her arms around them.

The light was very dim, cast by a few torches mounted down the long tunnel. Her eyes wandered around the cave, adjusting as she tried to see her surroundings.

She realized she wasn't alone. Across from her sat a woman who looked familiar to her. She opened her mouth to speak, but her attention was drawn to the footsteps to her left. A man was pacing back and forth, shaking his head wildly as he mumbled something unintelligible.

He moved his hands quite a lot, and he laughed at random

before striking himself on the side of the head. After he did that, he would go back to pacing again, shaking his head and mumbling.

Her mind raced as she watched him, although she was unable to see his features in the low light. A deep pit of worry formed in her stomach as he paced. It couldn't be! She refused to believe it.

"Arryn," he said, shaking his head again as he mumbled something else.

She only barely understood what he had said, but there it was—the evidence. When her name rolled off his lips, tears began to stream down her face. There was no doubting it.

That was her father.

Ten years. She had waited ten years to see him, and there he was. But it wasn't him… not really.

She opened her mouth, but another voice filled the small area. "Don't speak to him, Arryn. Not yet. We need to talk first."

Arryn looked at the woman sitting across from her, who was staring straight back. "Who are you?"

"I'm your cousin, Dana," she said.

Arryn's eyes widened as she realized just who she was. As children, they had lived only a couple houses from one another in the city. They had played together all the time with her friend Esther, who also lived on the street. She thought Dana was gone with the rest of her family.

"Have you been here the whole time?" Arryn asked. "With him?"

Dana nodded. "They captured me at the same time they took him, but I can't blame anyone for not noticing. I wasn't watched nearly as carefully as he and your mother were. They found us together. I had snuck out to meet him that night. We had a plan to save you, but it didn't go well. It was probably for the best, because Adrien would've found you eventually. They watched your father in hopes he would lead them to you."

"I don't know if you are aware of it or not, but Adrien is dead.

A girl named Hannah came through and wiped him off the map. Everyone who worked for him, too. I killed his daughter when she came back to get her revenge on the city," Arryn said.

Dana's eyes widened. "You killed Adrien's daughter? Talia? She's the very reason we're here. Your father found out about her, and Adrien didn't want anyone to know." The woman laughed. "If you went back to the city and took her out, you must be pretty damn strong."

"I had excellent teachers over the years while living in the Dark Forest. Celine is there now. We found each other in the city, and she's been living with me in the Forest of late. It's a long story, but I'm sure I'll be able to tell you about it later. Now, what's up with my father?"

Dana sighed as she looked at Christopher. "They've poisoned him with various things over the years. Mushrooms, belladonna —whatever comes along. They like to experiment on him with random plants. They keep him under, because when he's lucid, he begins to freak out about you."

Shaking her head, Arryn said, "I have to get him out of here. Both of you." She turned to her cousin. "Do you have magic?"

She laughed, but it was unamused. "I do, but not right now. They know I would never use my magic against them, because they would hurt him to get back at me. The guy that usually watches over us, Jace, he quit pumping me full of that shit for a while, but now that Alaric is back, they're forcing him to do it again. It's weak, so I'm still in my right mind, but I sure as hell can't focus enough to touch the magic."

Arryn knew exactly what she was talking about, because that was just how she felt as well.

"Your dad was just given another dose. He acts like that for quite a while after, but he should come around in a few hours. You know, I've learned a lot here. If what I heard was true, you have the power to heal him, yes?"

Arryn nodded. "Yes, but not right now. I'm just like you—I

don't have the ability to touch my magic. Someone would have to heal me before I could heal him."

Dana nodded. "Then my advice would be to act like you are out of it. Maybe they won't dose you again." She shrugged. "I don't know. But I do know our only chance of getting out of here lies with you. We have to find a way."

Arryn didn't speak again, but turned her attention back to her father and his non-stop pacing. She knew better than anyone that getting out of the cave would require her to reach her magic. She couldn't imagine the three of them dying here like that, and she wouldn't allow herself to be used as a weapon against the Dark Forest either.

She had to come up with a solution, and soon. After all, she *had* been in worse situations.

ALARIC WAS MAKING his way toward the cave when his brother stopped him. The two had decided to meet that morning, because Alaric wanted to introduce Jerick to his newest prisoner. He hadn't had the pleasure yet, and Alaric wanted to see that he did.

"How do you think this is going to go?" Jerick asked. "Do you think she'll do what we ask?"

Alaric nodded. "She's going to do just fine. After she realized the hold I have over her and what I would do to her father, she came around quite nicely. By now, she's probably realized I have her cousin, too."

Jerick nodded, his expression revealing his uncertainty. "Something about this just feels off. You said she was alone when you found her?"

Alaric sighed as he rubbed the bridge of his nose. "Yes. It was one of the things we anticipated. We knew the letter would get under her skin, and she would more than likely disobey Alexander. We knew she would either listen to him and stay put, which is why we went in the first place, or she would go rogue. Guess what happened? She went alone, which was much easier on us, obviously."

Shaking his head, Jerick said, "That's not what I mean. Think about it. How often do you see a druid of the Dark Forest without his or her familiar? *That's* what I'm asking. Animals might have been affected somewhat, but the smoke is deadlier on humans. So, if her familiar wasn't there—where was it?"

Alaric stared at his brother for a moment, running his conversation with Arryn through his head. "She mentioned walking through the Forest with her white tiger. I didn't really think about it at the time, but that must have been her familiar."

Jerick was obviously annoyed by hearing this. "Fantastic. That means she more than likely sent the beast back to warn the others. If she did, trouble might find us soon. You should have searched for the familiar, Alaric. This may have cost us."

Alaric shrugged. "And again, this is something we planned for. Maybe not directly, but we planned for the possibility the others were too strong to be affected by the smoke. That was why we were trying to lure Arryn out without having to go in after her. We'll be fine. And if not, you and I will take off and find another way into the Forest."

"You mean sacrifice our people to save ourselves?" Jerick asked.

Alaric laughed. "That's *exactly* what I mean. I'm not above threatening another army to follow me into battle. I wanted to take my people with me, but it's not necessary as long as I win."

Alaric clapped his brother on the back before leading him into the cave. It was time he met his special weapon.

CATHILLIAN WAS on the verge of exploding. It was taking everything Celine and Samuel had to keep him calm, so even Elysia and the Chieftain opted to stay out of his way as they traveled south through the Dark Forest.

Not only was Arryn missing, but now Corrine was as well, which Cathillian knew happened because they waited and rested up. Corrine was used to sneaking around. It was easy for her to eavesdrop on adult conversations she otherwise wouldn't be invited to hear.

He had no doubt she had gone south to find Arryn. While the others were confident they would find her on the way, he damn well knew better. That girl was faster in trees than people were on foot, even with horses. She moved like the *Schatten*, and she was just as fast.

Corrine would make it to Arryn long before they did, and she would more than likely die in the process, trying to do the one thing they should have done without question.

He understood his grandfather's reasoning, but he also hated him for it. If he lost Arryn because of his grandfather's rules and fears, he would never forgive the man. He would always love him, and stand by his side because he believed the Chieftain was a good man with a good heart, but he would never forgive him if he lost the person he loved most in the world.

"That lass has been through hell and back," Samuel said. "She's survived things I don't think any of us coulda. Give 'er some credit. Just ye watch. We're gonna run in there ta save the day, and she's gonna end up rescuin' all our arses."

Celine laughed. "It really is true. I know your mom and grandpa are strong, but Arryn..." She didn't need to finish the sentence. Everyone knew how it would have ended.

Arryn had continued to surprise everyone every day. With her capacity to love, defend, and teach, she had proven herself worthy of a title that had never been given to one so young.

"I'm aware of that," Cathillian said, "but that's not my only worry. When Corrine came here, Arryn took her in like she was her own, just like we did for her. She is incredibly important to

Arryn, and she's important to me, too. I let her get away, out of my sight. We all did, and now she's in danger. We lost Arryn, and we lost the person who is essentially her adopted daughter. Snow and Dante are both a mess, too. Did you see the cub before we left? He's completely lost without Arryn and Corrine. He's Arryn's familiar, but he's just as close to the girl. We have to find them."

"I'm sorry, lad," Samuel said as he looked at Cathillian with genuine sympathy. "We're gonna find 'em both, and they'll be safe when we do. And then we're gonna rip the balls off every one o' those bastards."

The druid nodded. "That's more fucking like it."

CHAPTER EIGHTEEN

Arryn looked away from Dana as she heard footsteps and swallowed hard as she felt the familiar dark energy coming closer. It was Alaric, but there someone else with him. She wondered if maybe it was Aeris.

She had hoped she would get the opportunity to see him again. Of course, she wanted to be at full strength when it happened, but she wanted to look into his eyes and see what she would find.

Instead, it was only Alaric and his brother, Jerick.

"Is the sun shining this morning?" Alaric asked, referring to their conversation the night before when he had initially called her "Sunshine."

She smiled, cocking her head to the side. "That depends. You lettin' me go this morning? How about dear old Dad?"

He laughed and looked at his brother. "See? I told you she's hilarious." He turned back to Arryn. "It's funny you should say that. My brother wanted to have a little talk with you before we do anything else, so we'll see how that goes."

Jerick stepped forward with a broad smile on his face and knelt several feet away. "See, last night you had a conversation with my brother and you mentioned a white tiger. That got me thinking… That tiger wasn't with you, now was it?"

Arryn swallowed hard, trying to fight back the bile. She had a feeling she knew where this was headed. "No, she wasn't. I needed to approach you alone. I had planned to sneak into the camp and liberate my father. There was no way I could've ridden a white tiger in here while trying to be stealthy." It was a partial lie, but she hoped he wouldn't catch it.

"Oh, *there* it is. Now, I expected you to say something like that, but here's the thing… I *distinctly* remember hearing something big roar. I haven't run into many jungle cats, so I just assumed it was Alexander's bear. But it wasn't, was it? Keep in mind that if I don't believe your answer, I'll cut one of your father's fingers off."

Arryn wanted to cry. While the darkness inside this man wasn't nearly as deep as Alaric's, he was far more terrifying. Finally, she shook her head. "No. It wasn't the bear. It was Snow."

Jerick smiled. "'Snow.' Pretty name for a white cat. That wasn't so hard, right? After all, being honest with each other is how friendships are formed, and my brother thinks the two of you can be friends. My next question... Did you send her to warn the others?"

Arryn didn't want to answer, but she knew she had no choice. She nodded. "Yes, I did. I told her to wake everyone she could and get them out of the village."

Jerick sighed, shaking his head at her in a disappointed manner. "That's what I was afraid of, but your honesty buys you a bit of leeway. Now comes the fun part." He turned to his brother. "We don't have long before Alexander and the others get here. Get their asses outside. It's time for the test."

Arryn's eyes widened as she looked at Dana. Both had fear and uncertainty in their expressions. Alaric called out, and six dark druids ran in and separated into pairs. Each pair grabbed one of them and lifted them roughly by the arms.

Arryn and Dana began kicking and fighting as they dragged

them out of the cave. The bright morning light hit Arryn's eyes, blinding her as they pulled her into the open. They threw her down, and she landed hard on her hands and knees.

Her body still felt weak, but she managed to struggle upright. When her eyes adjusted, she saw nearly a hundred dark druids gathered around the area as both dark chieftains looked at their attentive crowd.

"What is this? What's going on?" Arryn asked.

She unsteadily tried to get to her feet, but was immediately kicked back to her knees. She all but growled at the guilty druid as he came around to stand in front of her, but still far enough out of the way that she could see both Dark Chieftains.

Alaric held his hands out to the sides, smiling as he looked at the crowd before turning his gaze on her. "Why, this is your test, my *dear friend*. You see, we'll need to leave very quickly if your adopted family catch up to us. The question is, do we leave you behind to hopefully gain ground between us and them, or do we take you with us because you'll help us escape?"

Jerick smiled next to him, pointing a finger in the air. "Ah, don't forget the best part. If we have to leave you behind, clearly we'll have no use for you or your father…or your cousin for that matter. If you refuse to help us they *will* be killed, and it won't be pleasant. We'll leave you behind and take them with us. Then we'll send them to you piece by piece."

"Arryn, you can't do this," Dana said. Arryn turned to face her. "You can't help them take the Dark Forest. You know your dad would never want this. I don't either. Save yourself and save the Dark Forest, even if that means letting us die."

"Arryn."

Her eyes widened as she heard his voice speak her name. She turned her head in the opposite direction to see her father looking directly at her. There were questions in his eyes, but when he saw her, it seemed to bring him back to the present—even if only a little.

"Is that really you?" he asked.

"Aw! Isn't that cute? He's lucid enough to remember who she is," Jerick said. "Arryn, sweetheart, you can't let that man die after all you've been through, after all *he's* been through, can you? You've waited *ten years* to see him, and he's right there. That's your father, and you *can* have him back. All you have to do is help us take the Dark Forest."

Her father looked toward the two men standing ahead of them, his eyes suddenly clearer and his brows furrowed. Realization crossed his expression as he slowly began to shake his head.

He turned back to Arryn. "No. Don't. Save yourself. Your safety is all that has ever mattered to me. The Dark Forest gave you a home when I couldn't. Don't forsake it and everyone in it for me. You know better than that."

Her jaw dropped open as she tried to speak, but she couldn't. Tears streamed down her face. She began to sob when she heard her father, her *real* father, talking to her as he had when she was a child. As if no time had passed at all.

All she wanted in the world was to reach out to him, but it was just like it had been ten years ago.

If she reached out she would be pulled away all over again, not allowed to touch him.

"I don't know if this is a dream or not, but if you're real, don't do it. You've always been my angel. Don't let them turn you into a destroyer." Tears fell down her father's face as he stared at her.

She took a shaky, uneven breath and slowly nodded. "I love you, Daddy."

"I love you too, baby girl. Now do what's right."

She closed her eyes, forcing the last of her tears to fall down her cheeks as she faced forward. She wasn't ashamed of her emotion, and for the first time, she regarded it as more than just a weapon.

It was her strength.

"Well, darling?" Alaric said. "What is your decision?"

She risked one more look at her father, and he nodded. She turned to look at Dana, and without hesitation she did the same.

Taking a deep breath, she faced the Dark Chieftains again. "I will *never* help you. I will *never* help you take the Dark Forest. I would rather burn in hell."

Alaric smiled. "Wouldn't that be a fitting end, given that's exactly where you promised to send me?"

A wicked smile crossed her face. "The day's not over yet, sweet cheeks."

Jerick shook his head and rolled his eyes. "What a fucking waste of time and effort. I've had enough. Bring in her consolation prize. Show her exactly what *not* thinking about the consequences of her stupid decisions gets her."

Arryn heard a scream, and the voice was familiar—far too familiar. Corrine was thrown to the ground several feet in front of her, and the little girl had tears in her eyes as she looked from Arryn to her father.

"I'm sorry," she said, her tiny voice shaking. "I thought I could save you. I thought I could call vines from the trees and carry you and your father away, but all the trees here are dead. *Everything here is dead.*"

Arryn's hands covered her mouth as she shook her head, more tears falling. "It's me who's sorry. If I could have healed myself, I would've been able to save all of you. Remember what I taught you. Your emotions are your greatest weapon, not weakness. Even your fear."

Corrine's eyes widened for a moment before her expression fell again, more tears falling.

Despite her brave words to Corrine, for the first time in a long time, Arryn experienced a moment of doubt in herself. She had never allowed weakness to swallow her, but at that moment —poisoned and unable to touch her physical or magical strength —she was engulfed by doubt, by weakness.

Jerick stepped forward, laughing as he grabbed Corrine by the hair and roughly yanked her back, causing her to cry out again. "But she can't, little one! She *can't* save you. She can't save *any* of you. You failed, you little shit. I knew I should've killed you the day you were born. There was always something off about you. Your own *parents* didn't even want you."

"Stop it!" Arryn shouted, rage taking hold of her. "Leave her alone. If you want to torment someone come after me, but leave her be."

He leaned down and took out a knife, holding Corrine tightly by the hair with one hand while flipping the blade in the other, and movement to either side of her caught her attention. Dark druids were lifting swords over the necks of both Dana and her father.

"I changed my mind. I don't like long, drawn-out goodbyes," Jerick said coldly. "We're just going to end this now."

Arryn gasped, frozen as a debilitating and warring mixture of both fear and pure, unrelenting hatred took hold of her. She had no idea where to move, who to save as she saw the swords lifting higher and ready to swing down.

She could feel her magic deep inside her, but she still couldn't touch anything, even with the raging emotions flowing through her.

There was nothing she could do. She was about to watch all of them die, knowing they would kill her after.

But then, Corrine yelled. She heard the girl's voice echoing loud and strong through the area, but it didn't sound as terrified or fearful as a child her age should have sounded in her situation.

It sounded *pissed*.

Arryn looked at her, realizing Corrine had taken her lesson to heart as the little girl's eyes glowed vibrant green. Her hands flew out in front of her, and a wave of warm energy washed over Arryn as Corrine healed her.

The heat swept through her entire body, immediately dissipating the effects of everything they had done to her with the smoke and the tea. And because she had been trying so hard to touch her magic before, once she was healed enough to reach it, her eyes immediately flashed black and green.

A deep, ominous crack of thunder exploded overhead in the sky and clouds began to roll in. Both Chieftains' eyes widened as fear shot through them.

They had made a very grave mistake. They hadn't thought to poison the girl whom they believed had no *real* magic.

Jerick immediately let go of Corrine. The weakened girl fell to her hands and knees, but she was safe and alive.

"Do it! Do it now!" Aeris shouted as he came through the crowd. "Kill them all before she gets up!"

Arryn felt the shift of energy around her and turned just enough to see the swords began to swing down. Her entire body tensed as she flexed, a barrier exploding on either side of her to protect both Dana and her father.

The wind began to pick up as she slowly stood, and the nearly black clouds in the sky began to twist and turn. The first druid ran at her with a sword, but she twisted out of the way before jumping on his back and snapping his neck.

"Take her now!" Alaric shouted as she stood again.

She turned and pointed at him, smiling. "I'm coming for *you* next."

She threw her hands straight out in front of her and spun, and the resulting blast of wind sent dozens of dark druids flying backward.

She ran to her right, jumping and planting a foot hard in the gut of one and using the momentum to kick another before landing on her feet again. She picked up a sword and took the head off one druid before severing the arm of another.

They came at her and came again, but she was too fast. She heard that familiar voice—Aeris' voice—shouting as he tried to pull his sister free. She lifted her hands and a bolt of lightning crashed, killing several dark druids and scattering the rest.

She wouldn't last much longer at the rate she was going, but she would do everything she could to save her family.

The druids began to run in different directions, and she tried to find the Dark Chieftains. She couldn't see them in the crowd, but she did see one of her targets, and quickly located the other.

Raising her hand to the sky, she began to walk forward. "Oh, Aeris," she said in a singsong voice.

Somehow, her voice carried over the loud wind, and he stopped dead in his tracks, turning with wide eyes to face her. Her eyes turned an even darker green as she looked to the sky at the twisting clouds beginning to take shape.

"Get inside!" Arryn shouted to her father, Dana, and Corrine.

They jumped up and ran toward the cave as the swirling clouds began to drop. Jenna and Aeris ran in opposite directions to stay with the fleeing crowd, but it did no good. The thin but powerful funnel cloud touched down and pulled several inside, including Jenna and Aeris.

She took a deep breath, feeling the incredible energy sapping out of her. She dropped her hand, and the funnel cloud dispersed, throwing everyone inside in different directions.

Arryn picked up a sword from the ground, praying to the Bitch she could make it to them. She first found Jenna and placed her foot on the dark druid's neck. The girl was only barely alive at that point, but still lively enough to hear Arryn speak to her one last time.

"You nearly took Cathillian from me that day outside the city. I've been waiting for this moment ever since," Arryn said, her voice icy.

Jenna wrapped her hands around Arryn's boot as she tried to swallow and choked out between breaths, "You were never good enough for him, *Arcadian*."

Arryn laughed as she bent to look her in the face, her foot still on the girl's throat. "That's where you're wrong. He is everything I need, and I'm that for him, too. You never stood a chance, and you tried to kill him to prove it. This is for him—for *my* Cathillian."

Arryn straightened again, lifting her boot and bringing it down hard to crush the woman's throat. Aeris, whose back had broken when he fell from the twister, screamed loudly as he saw his sister die and tried to drag himself to her. Arryn stood in his way.

"And *you*!" Arryn exclaimed with bitterness and absolute hatred. "I wish I could kill *you* a thousand times. You are just as bad as Adrien. You spent a decade torturing my father. I would love to spend twice that repaying you for what you've done, but he taught me better than that. *Alexander* taught me better than that, too."

He laid there crying as he stared at her.

She sighed and shook her head. "I suppose only one death will have to suffice." And with that, she lifted the sword and brought it down on his neck, ending his life and her father's torture with it.

Arryn heard someone screaming her name, and she turned to see her family running toward her. She took a few steps, smiling like a little kid before her eyes rolled back in her head and she dropped to her knees, unconscious.

Everyone had gathered around the firepit as they always did after a hard day. Arryn was still exhausted, even after sleeping the whole way back to the safest secluded parts of the Dark Forest. She yawned as she left her house and began the short walk to join them.

"Need some company?" Cathillian asked before pinning her against a tree and placing his hands gently on either side of her face as he kissed her.

She moaned a little as she returned the kiss, wrapping her arms around him and hauling him even closer. After a few moments, he pulled away and exhaled heavily. "Wow. I wasn't expecting all that."

She smiled. "Well, I'm just glad to be back and have the opportunity."

He quirked an eyebrow at her. "What? That almost sounds like you like me."

She shrugged. "Maybe just a little."

"Mmhmm. Let's not forget, the moment you saw me you wrapped your arms around me and called me *your* Cathillian. *I* sure won't forget it."

She rolled her eyes. "I was delirious and half-conscious. And trust me, I *know* you won't ever forget it."

Cathillian looked at her incredulously.

She sighed. "Okay, okay, so I might have called you 'my Cathillian' just before I killed Jenna. Clearly, I was dreaming about it."

He smiled and kissed her again. "Boy, look at you. *So* clingy. Gross!"

She pinched his side, and they both laughed. Pulling away, she groaned at the loss of the heat and comfort in his eyes, and pouted at him for good measure. He extended his hand, and though she took it, she didn't seem happy about it.

"I just want to go back to sleep," she said.

"Well, I wasn't going to tell you, but we have a surprise," he said with a smile. "And maybe afterward I'll give you a massage."

Her left brow raised as she looked at him with curiosity. "You had me at surprise, but massage? Absolutely."

He gave an exaggerated nod. "You've been asleep for the past three days, and the Chieftain and my mother have both been working on your father. Zoe has as well. He still has a long way to go, but he wants to see you."

Arryn's eyes lit up and a smile spread across her face. She had wanted to see her father for the last few days, but he hadn't been ready for her.

He had felt embarrassed that he couldn't keep his mind straight, and now all he wanted in the world was to have a coherent conversation with his daughter.

He had asked the Chieftain to help him get better. He wanted to look at his daughter and see who she had become, not the little girl he still saw because his mind had been frozen in time.

And Christopher wanted her to see her real father, not the mess he had been with the dark druids.

He still didn't understand exactly how he had managed to be lucid the day she had freed them, but everyone guessed it was from the spike of adrenaline caused by laying his eyes on his baby girl—a daughter he hadn't even been sure was alive any longer.

Cathillian nodded. "I've been hanging out with him, and he's an amazing guy. You know, I never imagined meeting someone who loves his family as much as we do here, but he sure as hell does. After all this time, your dad's back."

She sighed, smiling. "Does this mean I have to quit telling dick jokes?"

Cathillian laughed. "No, it's fine. I've already prepared him a bit. I told him what you did with Chippy and Nutty. He seems to think you're *hilarious*." He sighed and shook his head. "I don't know why. You're just mean."

She chuckled and playfully punched him in the arm. "Wouldn't it be funny if I got that quality from him? I bet a *lot* of my sense of humor came from him. This could be great."

He groaned. "Great indeed. Now I'll have two of you instructing the squirrels to fill my house with nuts."

Arryn saw her father at the firepit talking to the Chieftain and Elysia. He stood so much taller now. His hair had been cut, and he had shaved. He looked just as he had years ago.

"Dad?" Arryn said cautiously.

Christopher turned to her, his eyes almost twinkling in the firelight as his smile grew. He rushed to his daughter and wrapped his arms around her, holding her tightly.

"You are *everything* your mother and I hoped for. I couldn't have specified anyone better if I had tried. I love you so much," he said, tears in his voice.

She breathed through her own emotion and when she inhaled, he smelled just like he used to when he hugged her. He smelled like home, somehow exactly the same, and it brought on a wave of emotion she wasn't sure she was ready for. She welcomed it anyway.

"I love you too, and I'm so happy to have you back. Welcome home," she said, feeling an overwhelming sense of peace for the first time in a long time. Everything was exactly as it should be—minus the impending war, of course.

She pulled away, and wiped away her tears, turning to look at the Chieftain and Elysia. "I know I should be the last person in the world to want to talk about this right now, and really, I am. But it doesn't change the fact that it needs to be discussed. Alaric and Jerick got away, and so did most of the dark druids. How are we going to deal with this?"

"Maybe we can help with that," a young woman said from behind them as another one climbed down from her back.

Everyone jumped into a defensive position and each woman lifted her hands in the air, signaling peace.

"Who are you, and what do you want?" the Chieftain asked.

The one who had been carrying what was obviously her twin sister smiled. "I'm Bast, and this is Cleo. Long story short, we come from far away, and when we reached Arcadia, we met Amelia. She said we needed to come here and ask someone named Arryn for help."

"She also said to mention that I damn near died saving a rearick named Ren, and you guys know him," Cleo said.

Arryn looked at Samuel , who had started paying close attention after that name was mentioned. Ren was one of his close friends, and Cathillian had spent quite a bit of time healing Ren and his men after they were attacked by remnant.

Arryn took several steps forward, separating herself from the crowd. "I'm Arryn. Amelia sent you to me?"

Cleo nodded. "She said you have a war brewing just now, and that we should hang out in Arcadia and wait until it passed." She smiled as she looked at her sister and back at Arryn with confidence. "I told her, 'Fuck that!' We need your help, but I'm sure as hell not gonna ask for it if I don't offer you something in return."

Arryn's eyes narrowed as she looked her over. She could see a few spots of blood on her shirt, though it didn't look terrible. "And what do you have to offer us?"

"Like we said, we think we can help. Only thing is, I have a big gash from shoulder to rib that I need healed before we fight anyone. Your guard boys are out there on horses racing here right now. My sister not only jumped over your fancy little fence, but outran them on foot with me on her back, so I'm pretty sure we're qualified. Interested?"

A smile spread across Arryn's face as she looked over her shoulder. The Chieftain and Elysia both looked rather impressed, and they nodded.

Arryn turned back and gazed at them speculatively, her arms crossed over her chest. "Sure. Let's see what ya got."

FINIS

Well, look at me! Forgetting to do author notes!

Right now—well, until Steve reminded me about doing this important part!—I'm editing the first book in a BRAND NEW Age of Magic series! The author's name is P.J. Cherubino, and I'm in love with the lead character, Astrid. I really think you guys will get into it. Plus, the book, well—said in Deuce Bigalow style—it's a *huge* bitch! So, lots to enjoy.

Other than that, I'm watching my three-year-old niece playing with my brand-new kitten.

A bit about kitty: He is *fucking adorable*—a cute, chubby, fuzzy-as-hell, long-haired black kitten named Buford. I also call him Baby Boombalatti, after my much larger also black, also fuzzy, twenty-pound cat, whose real name is Korra, but I enjoy nicknames, in case you didn't figure that out by reading about Monsieur Buttpuff (the snow rabbit) in book three.

I love my tiny little black kitten, but I must say I'm not a fan of his murder-toes... He likes to use them to climb up my leg. *Screams*

Back to the niece: She stayed the night with me last night, and she's just precious. She's also quite the trouble-maker (just like her mother). I watch her play now, and listen to how smart she is, and see how funny she is already, and all I can think is…

"Oh, shit… It's another Amanda… She's going to be a master prankster, and I'm never going to feel safe again."

Her mother, my loving BABY sister, is the type who will drive thirty minutes out of the way to grease your door handles, or use her spare key to take something out of your house that you were supposed to be watching for her, so she can deviously watch you sweat a bit while thinking you lost it…

I love my niece. BOTH of those girls. Aside from my boys, they are my absolute everything.

And onto book stuff!

Here it is, the start of Arc Two—which will only be two books, by the way. Then on to bigger stuff! I can't believe that I started this journey back in March, and I just *couldn't* wait to get the first one out. It was another four months that I had to wait to do it because the start of my series required the first Arc for Chris and Lee to wrap up, but look at us now!

I have already outlined and started on the next book, and I am super excited about it.

Oh! And speaking of excitement… It's November 17th right now, twenty-five days post The Deceiver release date, and it's STILL at 100% Five Star reviews…

Uh—*fuck yes!* Thank you! I'm always grateful for the wonderful reviews that you guys leave, but seeing that all those reviews are positive just totally makes it all worth it.

Speaking of those reviews—I always ask you a question and ask that you leave the answer in a review. It gives me an idea of who you are and what you're like. Some of you I see responding consistently, and that's awesome. I love the opportunity to read a little about you, too!

So, last time, I asked if there was someone in your life that really pushed you toward your dream. I received a lot of replies and learned a lot of you had amazing support and love from family/friends, and I even learned what some of you aspired to be.

Opens The Deceiver Amazon page to name drop

- Kelly O'Donnell: I'm glad your granny supported you so much! They seem to have a way with it a lot of times, and its special for sure. You and I have talked a bit, and you are amazing —so I definitely think she would be proud. *winks*

- Dan Coursen: Singing is awesome! I used to want to be a singer, too! When I told my grandmother, she tried to support it however she could. Like yours, my parents weren't too supportive of it, but hey, it never stopped me! I'm glad that never stopped you either—even if neither one of us made a career out of it.

And Finally, Pam Moore: Engineering school! That's so awesome! Pam said, "My mother drove me to go to engineering school, which I did. Loved the field and retired from it. My dad helped me through school, and I was able to thank them both." – That is just awesome.

It's shocking how many kids have to put themselves through school (and I don't mean financially—that's very common these days here in the States—but they have no emotional support). My oldest son is CONSTANTLY bringing me new things he drew/wrote in his comic books, and I keep telling him that I'm going to send him to art/film/graphics school one day. Whatever it is that he chooses out of those, I'll find a way. Somehow, it'll happen.

He will never be the business school type. He will never be the management type. He's an artist! Brandon has displayed interests in art, movies, video games (and their creation—his comic books are actually for his "game" he's designing at eleven years old), and even robotics and architecture. So, I'm already expecting to spend a lot on either art school of some kind or engineering.

Thanks so much for the reviews, please keep leaving them. Not only do they help the books (mine and others) but I truly do enjoy reading and learning about you guys, which is why I like to share things with you about myself as well!

For your next question review assignment: What talents/dreams do your kiddos (or nieces/nephews/grandchildren/etc.) have, and do you have anything special you do to push them?

Until next time! <3

P.S. For your Amusement

Bitch and Bastard...

It has already begun! I heard a sweet, innocent "At Tandy" (Aunt Candy) from my niece... I turned to my left with a smile and proceed to nearly shit my pants. She's holding a fake cockroach in her hand, not two inches from my face. Laughing maniacally, she just leaves it on the arm of my chair and walks away to return to the kitten.

I screamed... like a bitch... Oh, goodness. No one judge me—but you can judge her if you want. She's mean! She's a toddler Arryn!

First, thank you for not only reading this story, but making it through *An Tandy's* Author Notes to read mine, as well.

Right now, I'm riding in a car going from Dallas-Fort Worth, Texas to Las Vegas, Nevada. We might have made it fairly quickly, had that cop outside of Amarillo, Texas not pulled me over.

I have to admit that I was driving for the first four hours, and had pretty much resigned myself to getting a ticket on such a long trip. Not because I wanted a ticket, but I knew I was going to be ...uh... driving with the *flow of traffic* and when leaving that Buc-ee's back in Roanoke, Tx it just felt like it was 'my time,' you know?

It's been a few years since I've received a ticket on the freeway for speeding and for whatever reason, it felt like I was going to be culled from the herd (lots of Texas speak, here) and given the Texas DPS brand.

I know, they call it a citation, but it is a 'pay up' notice for the local township.

Now, I don't know that I was speeding because I wasn't paying attention to the speedometer when I noticed the occifer (yes, I spelled that incorrectly on purpose) come over from the other side of the highway and cross the median to turn around and speed up. Then passing the person behind me to grace me with his presence with great fanfare!

You know, those 'look at me – look at me!' lights in red and blue no the top of his car?

<SIGH!>

I really didn't want to play with the occifer at all, so I provided the necessary documentation after a few 'yes sirs' and 'no sirs' and otherwise stayed quiet.

Now, I have to answer to the court within two weeks. The court is FAR away from anywhere I live so that's a major PITA. Time for me to figure out how to deal with citations that come from cities in the Texas panhandle.

I'd preferred he scared me with a fake roach.

For the record, I pulled WAY off the road, mostly into the grass so the officer wouldn't be near the traffic when he got out of his vehicle.

While I'm not happy with a ticket, DPS officers certainly deserve our respect for their efforts.

The officer who desired a moment (or twenty) of my time was at least ten or more years my senior, and I'm fifty. I can't imagine what he has seen in his career on the roads that might make me have problems sleeping at night.

On another note, we are officially in the 'November to December struggle.' What I mean by this is we Indie authors / publishers are in between Thanksgiving and Christmas where the Traditional publishers are selling a serious amount of books.

For us indies who don't sell many paperbacks in stores (or practically none like us) we will be selling against the headwind of Christmas. Our ranks will go down as those authors with Traditional publishers go up and this steady headwind continues until about two weeks after Christmas day.

A lot of Indie authors will hold off publishing until after this time. So naturally, I'm releasing on Christmas day.

Cause I'm stupid that way. Or contrarian, whatever ways sounds better in a press release!

Over Thanksgiving, I spoke with all three of our boys, and while two are published authors, the last was definitively a 'no way' when we spoke last. This Thanksgiving while he was at home, he wrote 4,000 words in two days, and I think just maybe I might get three little authors.

Oh, OH! AND the Author's wife read my first book in The Kurtherian Gambit (Death Becomes Her) and liked it!

We have officially moved into a new dimension; I hope you all made it over here with me!

Ad Aeternitatem,

Michael Anderle

p.s. – I should have led off with my wife reading book 01 of The Kurtherian Gambit, but the occifer was preoccupying my thoughts.

TALES OF THE FEISTY DRUID

with Michael Anderle

The Arcadian Druid (01) - The Undying Illusionist (02) - The Frozen Wasteland (03) - The Deceiver (04) - The Lost (05) - The Damned (06) Into The Maelstrom (07)

THE THERIAN CHRONICLES

with Amanda Browning

The Dark Professor (1) The Therian Prince (2)

BOOKS BY MICHAEL ANDERLE

For a complete list of books by Michael Anderle, please visit

www.lmbpn.com/ma-books/

All LMBPN Audiobooks are Available at Audible.com and iTunes. For a complete list of audiobooks visit:

www.lmbpn.com/audible